D0311758

Everwhere

Printed by www.Lulu.com

©2008 by Anna López Dekker

Cover design: Anna López Dekker

Illustrations: Anna López Dekker

ISBN 978-1-4092-0318-6

Library of Congress Control Number: 2008903996

No part of this book may be reproduced in any form, by print, photography, microfilm or any other means without written permission of the author

To Camille. Because you believed in me before I did.

And to Laia, Sara, Irene, Aina, Cèlia and Alba; may you

always have all the strength you need to overcome

any obstacle you find on your path.

Acknowledgements

There are quite a few people without whose support you might not be reading this book today.

First and foremost, Rob; this whole thing started with you wanting to produce a picture book, which I was going to write. Too bad this couldn't continue being a joint venture.

Just as important are the people who read my very first draft and actually liked it: Camille, Brian, Victoria, your positive reactions were just the encouragement I needed to go on.

Also Mum. The first thing you said when you finished reading was "I am pleasantly surprised". Coming from you, that is a compliment indeed; I hope this version will be an even more pleasant surprise.

Then there is Patsy Jones, who very kindly volunteered to edit and spent hours focusing on the nitty-gritty and making sure this book is actually readable.

And last, but not least, Jimmy. Without your encouragement when it came to that last hurdle, I might never have taken it. Or I might, but I'd probably have made something of a mess of it.

Thank you all you guys, from the bottom of my heart.

I really couldn't have done it without you.

1

It could have been a perfectly ordinary town: houses, streets, lampposts, parks and nice little patches of grass kids would have loved playing football on had the dogs not got to them first.

It was old, but not old enough to contain any ruins or even any remotely interesting buildings. Quite a few of the houses had been built in another century, but most, if not all of them had afterwards been adapted to the current times and in the process, many of them had lost much of their former seasoned look. There was a pretty, relatively old church, a sweet little town square where, on warm days, people liked to sit and chat, one or two nice shopping streets with more no-brand stores than ordinary and a rather bigger park than one would normally expect in a place like that, though nothing spectacular either. There wasn't a castle, a city wall or an old monastery; there weren't even any manors or old country houses. History had passed by, hardly touching the town at all; it was, and had always been, the kind of place where nothing ever really happens[1].

On the other hand, it was undeniably a pretty place; the houses, which sported a variety of soft colours, were all fresh looking and in good repair; the flowers on the window sills bloomed gaily, the streets were clean, the gardens well kept. On the whole, one could easily perceive that, despite its apparent lack of historical and cultural interest, the inhabitants had pride in their town.

And then, there was its location, near some of the most popular beaches in the country and at a convenient distance to pretty much

---

[1] Not that that can't be said for most places. Fortunately, or maybe not, history tends to leave its mark only in a few chosen places, leaving the rest untouched.

Which suits most people very well; adventure is far from being in everybody's blood.

everything, including two major cities, a famous sports stadium and a popular racing track.

All things considered, you couldn't blame people for thinking it was just another quaint, yet normal little town. Nothing special, just the kind tourists come to spend the day in when the weather isn't warm enough for the beach but too good to stay indoors, "ooh" and "aah" about and then leave the natives to take their walk in at evening.

It would definitely have been the most ordinary, every day, normal town in the world if it hadn't also contained the only door to Everwhere a human being could get through. Except, of course, (almost) no one knew about that.

2

Aside from her somewhat unusual name, Ythoda Newyew [2] was just the kind of kid one would expect from that town: ordinary. Nice, but ordinary.

In fact, despite being the only (un) known human being who knew her way into and around Everwhere (for as much as possible-the place is a maze and you don't always know where the path you take every day is going to lead to this time), she could indeed have won a contest for the most normal kid in town.

She was the kind of child who did well enough in school, but not so well as to be considered "uncool" or "nerdy" and only because she had to. She was a friendly girl who got along with a lot of people, had quite a few friends and, just like any girl her age, had acquired one or two sworn enemies.

She was generally well behaved, but did manage, like any self-respecting youngster, to get in trouble every how and then; but it is only

---

[2] No, that wasn't due to some tasteless joke of her parents. They were actually quite nice people with not much sense of humour at all.

The one to blame was her uncle, the unmarried younger brother of Ythoda's mother, a man with no known source of income but who spent most of his life travelling around (you know the kind, every family has one). He had come up with the name, and convinced his sister and her husband that "Ythoda" (pronounced eye-thaw-dah) meant "great wise woman" in ancient proto-Hungarian, or something like that.

Why her parents never checked up on it has ever remained a mystery. Ythoda has forgiven her uncle, though she never will tell him so, especially because, probably out of guilt, he has a habit of bringing her back expensive presents every time he goes on one of his trips. Or with other words: quite often.

Well, you can't blame a kid for making the most of a not-so-good situation, can you?

fair to say that in most occasions, that was due to a lack of sense of humour on the part of the adults who got annoyed with her.

Her tongue could be sharp, as could her sense of justice, but she never went so far as to alienate people; for all her lack of diplomacy, she was endowed with a measure of charm big enough to keep others from getting angry for longer than a little while.

She was pretty, or would be some day, in the girl-next-door kind of way "ordinary" is all about; she was of average height and build, but her budding figure showed quite some promise. She had pleasantly regular features with bright blue-green eyes and with a few freckles, which most people found "cute" but she herself tended to hate.

She was kind to her friends and sometimes nasty to her enemies[3]. And aside from a quite annoying fondness for climbing trees [4], her parents could not have wished for a nicer daughter.

There were only two things about her that would warrant more than fleeting attention from a stranger: her long, bright red hair, which despite her mother's entreaties she refused to wear down, and a certain aura of strength that would have been hard to miss were it not that people generally don't tend to see such things in a child Ythoda's age. Still anyone who really bothered to look at her could see that she would one day be an imposing woman, someone to take into account.

---

[3] Only when they absolutely asked for it- and an enemy can ask for nastiness in a surprisingly large number of ways. Just existing is often a very effective one.

[4] For parents who let their daughter go through life with the name "Ythoda", they had pretty fixed ideas on what girls are and aren't supposed to do.

3

It was that brat of a Frank who did it, really, as was only to be expected since no one else, and definitely no one in her right mind, would have come up with such a dangerous idea. Except that to Frank, danger had never been more than an abstract concept with no bearing on himself whatsoever. Which would explain how he could even have considered getting her into, well, this thing he got her into.

Of course, he had never existed in the first place; he was a figment of Ythoda's imagination. A twin brother figment, to be precise.

Yes, Frank was Ythoda's imaginary twin brother, the one she had dreamed up when her parents finally got it through to her that they really, truly weren't planning on any more offspring. She had then decided that, seeing as she really didn't see how she could go on living without a sibling to share her hare-brained schemes with[5], it was going to be up to her to provide one for herself; if that meant spending the rest of her life with an imaginary sibling, well, who was to blame but her parents? After

---

[5] Well, of course, she did have friends. More than enough of them too. It just so happened that they, like all of their parents and pretty much everybody in town, were of the down-to-earth, sensible kind that wouldn't be caught dead indulging in any fantastic game of make believe, at least not if it didn't include princesses and stepmothers or superheroes and villains. Ythoda, on the other hand, had a perplexing preference for concocting the most impossible situations and would always want to play them out in the most physical manner possible, never mind if it included such dangerous ventures as climbing into every tree in the surroundings, crossing the street at a run just as the city bus turned the corner and ever so many other ways of getting seriously hurt.

So on the one hand, it was not so surprising that, as time wore on, all of her friends stopped agreeing to play her games. On the other hand, it was their loss…

all, if they had only done their parental duty by her, she wouldn't have had any need to spend so much time in a world of her own…

After thinking long and hard, she had decided on a brother because she thought that then she would have someone to blame when she got into one of her scrapes with the boys.

She had decided on a twin because it's generally known that younger brothers are by definition annoying spoiled brats whereas older ones are always mean bullies. A twin brother is the only kind a girl can expect to have any measure of control over (not that it worked in Frank's case, but one is always free to dream).

She had decided on the name "Frank" to make up for her own name- although she had forgiven her parents and uncle, she never stopped wishing for a nice, normal name. She quite liked "Mary".

So, Ythoda dreamed up Frank and, just as she had intended, led him into every adventure she could imagine, which was quite a few of them, as her imagination had always been one of her strongest talents. She was one of those people who are able to "see" pretty much everything with their mind's eyes and she had a sense of magic that went well beyond what is considered generally acceptable in this society of ours. In fact, there had been a point where her continued belief in fairies and such things had begun worrying the adults around her[6]; there even had been talk about getting her "help", which she, being neither mad nor stupid, had taken as a sign to keep her ideas to herself. That had been the main reason to come up with Frank, because, not surprisingly, he would never have a problem with any of her fantasies, as long as they were fun. Which they were: together, they explored the whole world, such as Ythoda thought it should be[7], had the most exciting (and, when she got too carried away,

---

[6] The usual: parents, relatives, teachers, in short, all those people who are always trying to get the older kids to live in "the real world", all the while forgetting that reality often is what you make it.

Besides, why would younger kids be allowed to believe in Santa and older ones not in fairies? Talk about unfair!

[7] As in criss-crossed all over with tunnels that took them from one side to the Earth of the other in a matter of minutes, with every convenience Ythoda liked available to them with no extra charge and peopled not only with all of her heroes and idols, but also with all those fairy tale characters a girl her age had no business believing in any more, according to the powers that be.

sometimes even scary) experiences and met every kind of people, as well as beings.

Eventually, though, it was Frank who led his sister to a place she could never ever even have dreamed about; a place where not only everything you imagine comes true, but also where every "what if" and "but what about" and "I just wish" (these last ones are the most dangerous, by the way) actually happens.

Frank, being imaginary, came from Everwhere and that is how he could show Ythoda the door. He also guided her around as well as he could, for one can never really know one's way in Everwhere.

It just isn't that kind of place

4

Now, after reading all of the above, you might be thinking that Everwhere is just one more of those places that every child knows and then forgets about as she grows up.

Nothing is further from the truth. In actual fact, if there was ever a place that was not for kids, that's Everwhere.

It's not a place for adults either. It's not a place for people, that is, real people, at all.

Yes, of course, it might sound fun to be in a place where every wish comes true; after all, who wouldn't want to live a life of luxury and leisure, surrounded by everybody you wish, all of them doing exactly what you want them to? Or, if that is not your thing, you could go and do everything you've only ever dreamed of because it was too expensive, or too dangerous, or just plain not possible. And then, of course, there would be the little matter of becoming anything you wished to be, from a famous athlete or artist to the world's most prominent mathematical genius. So why not go ahead and let everybody know how to get to the Land-where-dreams come true? After all, everybody should have a right to receive her heart's wish...

Except for the fact that, even on the best of days, wishes are pretty treacherous things. For instance, how many times have you ever said, "I wish I were dead", without ever really meaning it? And that is only one of the obvious ones; there are many more potentially dangerous wishes; and the more innocuous a wish seems, the less likely it is to be safe, for yourself and for others[8]. In fact, one might even say that the

---

[8] Guess I got you there, huh? Bet you would never have thought of the consequences your wishes would have for others.

Well, think again, they would. Nothing in this world is ever without effect, so there.

only wishes without consequences are the ones you can achieve yourself without help from magic, luck or whatever it is you choose to believe in, which would make travelling to Everwhere pretty much beside the point.

Now you are probably thinking that this is all just preaching for the sake of it, that all that has been said above is just a way to keep people from wanting to go there. Besides that, you probably are a very smart person who could easily learn to control your thoughts so you won't wish for things you don't really want[9]. Or, if what you want is really that important, at least make sure those things would not have an adverse effect on others.

But even if that worked, there are other people's wishes to take into account as well; how would you like to be in a place like Everwhere when someone wished you were dead?

And what about all of everybody's nightmares, every fear of every person on Earth, every possibility ever imagined by anyone? (some people have a very dark imagination)

Enough said...

Besides, this story is not about why one should be careful about what one wishes for. There are plenty of stories that tell you just that. The point of this little digression is to show why Everwhere is not like fairy-tale places like Neverland, Candyland, Toyland, or whatever other something-land you've ever heard of or imagined (though, of course, all of the above, and a few more, actually exist in Everwhere).

The point is to show why there should never have been a door into it.

But there was a door.

No one knows how it came into existence. It could hardly have been created by an Everwhere creature; generally speaking, they didn't even know of the world that had spawned their own and the only ones who did knew better than to establish a connection between the two realities. Wishes and dreams could have done it, of course, but, even if someone in our reality had known about the place and foolishly wanted to visit it, the energy released in the process would have caused the gate

---

[9] Think again...

to be discovered and undone by the Wardens of the Land[10] before anybody even found out about its existence.

It must have been something very powerful to create the passage at all and even more to make it invisible to Powers and Wardens first and impossible to destroy afterwards- and it wasn't for lack of trying! (But we won't go into this now; maybe in a later story. Or maybe it can all be left to your imagination; knowing Everwhere, that would actually do the trick just fine).

Whatever had happened to create it, the fact is that the door actually went unnoticed for quite a while until Frank stumbled across it. It had been the strangest thing: one moment, he had been walking along a dirt path on a hill with only more hills in the distance[11], and the next there was a door slam in the middle of the way. He could have gone around it quite easily, as it was just a door standing there, with no house or anything behind it. But he had chosen to go through instead, through a gate that hadn't existed a moment before.

Of course, he himself had existed in Everwhere from the moment Ythoda began thinking of him, even though she hadn't been able to see him at first because he wasn't really here in our world. The appearance of the door had coincided with a time when she had been feeling that just imagining wasn't enough. Her friends, who, even though they had always been reluctant to join her in her particular brand of imaginary games, had still been keen on playing games of make-believe and had at times even consented to joining hers, were reaching the stage where they wanted to pretend they didn't want to pretend any more[12]. Therefore, they were less and less willing to go along with her, so Ythoda was beginning to feel a bit lonely for not being able to share her world of

---

[10] Nowhere is a real chaos. Everwhere isn't. There are laws there, natural and written ones, which prevent the place from blowing up from too much paradox. There are Powers in Everwhere, which were created by human imagination, like most else in the land. And these Powers created the Wardens, beings who are the complete opposite of imagination and thus are not affected by the constant change in Everwhere. Their job is to keep the inhabitants of the land (alive and not) in and humans out. They are usually very good at it, but they did make the one mistake once.

[11] Which goes to show that even a place made of imagination, like Everwhere is, can be as boring as a school on Monday.

[12] And then we wonder why growing up gets so confusing…

dreams with anybody any more. That was why now, more than ever, the need for a brother, a real one, was becoming almost an ache.

Come to think of it, it must have been the strength of Ythoda's wish for a brother that led him to the door; after all, she did have a particular kind of strength that went beyond either the physical or the rational.

Or, maybe it was Frank who had had some hidden power of his own, although how that would get him somewhere he didn't know existed is hard to imagine.

But, whatever the reason, he found the gate and also found a way to get through before the Wardens could prevent it.

It didn't take Frank long to find Ythoda in her world; it is often said that there is a special connection between twins and in their case it was definitely true. As soon as he crossed the gate, Frank was drawn to his sister like iron to a magnet; in fact, it was a good thing no one but her was, or ever would be, able to see him, as the sight of a boy flying upright towards an unknown destination would, no matter how puzzled his expression, have wrecked havoc with the nerves of a good many people.

Surprisingly, Ythoda took his sudden appearance at her doorstep, just when she was going out to play, in very good stride; she hardly even evinced any surprise at all. When he told her who he was she just nodded as if she'd known all along and didn't ask any questions; she just took his hand and dragged him along to her special place in the park. There they played. Ythoda was too overjoyed to even wonder where her brother had come from, or where he had been before he appeared or how it was possible for him to be there at all.

And Frank? For quite some time when he first came in the "real" reality- though who is to say what reality really is- he never even thought about the door or about Everwhere at all. He was just having too much fun.

Until the day Ythoda's imagination ran dry.

5

The children were playing in the park that day. Their favourite game lately had been to pretend they were cast away on a desert island, cut off from civilisation and everyone they knew. They had spent several exciting weeks exploring the island, building themselves a series of increasingly complex huts (partly imagined, partly real; even Ythoda couldn't live in an altogether imaginary world), fishing, hunting and learning which plants were edible and which were not. Of course, Ythoda paid for that last survival skill with more than one belly-ache but both she and Frank readily agreed that it was worth it if it meant they now knew exactly which berries in the park were meant for people to eat, and that grass really doesn't make a very nice soup in the long run.

Later on, of course, when the excitement of being the new Robinson Crusoes faded, the island turned out not to be deserted at all. The kids had met pirates of all kinds, cannibals who turned out to be allergic to human flesh, princesses from another island who had been brought to their one as an offering to a sea monster who then had to be fought (and beaten, of course), and, as the story progressed, even aliens from outer space[13] who had invited the children to take a tour of the Milky Way with them and visit their home galaxy afterwards.

That was where the trouble started, because Frank didn't feel like flying all the way to Andromeda, so they had to stay on their island. And it was then that Ythoda couldn't think of anything new to add to the game. In fact, she had become so upset at not being able to explore space that she couldn't think of any game at all- except for the alien one which Frank absolutely refused to play.

---

[13] Cute little pink ones. Ythoda was a girl after all.

Imaginary beings have no imagination. Everything is fact to them.

That is probably why the only thing Frank could come up with when the responsibility to invent a game fell to him was Everwhere.

In his memory, it was a fun place to be. During his life there, he had explored lots of places, some of them even more than once[14] and met a lot of different people, which might seem a very dangerous thing for a kid to do. But that wasn't the case for him; he never ran into any serious trouble because his sister, who, naturally, had been the author of all his experiences, had never willed it to be so. Also, for the same reason, every one of his ventures had had a happy ending, just as his sister liked.

In short, he had done, on his own, everything Ythoda and he did together later; adventure came effortlessly to him, as all he had to do in both worlds was to let his sister's imagination carry him along.

The Land's inhabitants don't have any enemies, natural or otherwise, unless both they and their enemies are part of the same figment of a mind; Ythoda had never imagined any enemies for her brother or for herself for that matter. So he had been able to roam free and interact with anybody or anything he liked without any danger to himself.

And because of that, he didn't realise that it could be very different for his sister; it was not only that before she created her brother, she had imagined herself in quite dire straits more than once, and that they could easily find themselves in those situations again[15], it was also

---

[14] There is nothing so fickle as human imagination, which is why Everwhere is subject to constant change. Luckily, it's mostly only the details and the inhabitants are quite used to waking up with a different hair colour every day.

It only gets problematic when the changes are so great as to make people wonder about their identities. Of course, if they lived in our world, they wouldn't think twice about that.

[15] Places, people, situations appear in Everwhere all the time, but they don't disappear quite as easily. As long as they stay in their creator's mind, no matter how deep in her subconscious, they remain in place, though they might become distorted or fade. Only when something is completely forgotten does it disappear entirely.

Unless it has been taken over by another imagination, which has an entirely different set of consequences.

that she did have enemies in her world, some of whom had wished her rather ugly things. Besides which, not being a figment of anybody's mind (in her world at least), she could, unlike Frank, stumble into a situation that hadn't been created for her and that fact could be a danger in itself.

If he had thought of any of that, he would never have brought her to his native land.

But he did.

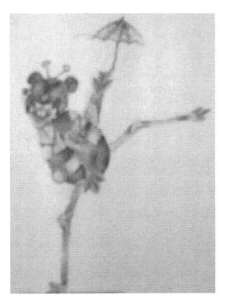

6

The door to Everwhere happened to be in the park they always played in. Of course that sounds like too much coincidence, but you must remember that Everwhere doesn't work like our world. Coincidence doesn't really exist there, everything happens for a reason, even if there isn't really one.

In this case, Frank could have found the door only if it led him to Ythoda. It did. Was the door caused by Ythoda's wish being stronger than the laws of the Land? Perhaps so, but it might as well have been something else. By now, it should be clear that its existence must have had everything to do with Ythoda; the question is what "everything" means.

It wasn't one of those magic doors in trees or walls, doors which open if you know the exact spot to touch. It wasn't an invisible door that would open if you traced it in the air during a full moon. It wasn't any kind of door a human would have thought of, even though only a human or an Everwhere inhabitant could go through it.[16]

It was just an old wooden door hanging askew in a fence that surrounded a meadow in the park where, for some reason, someone had once put some sheep. It was one of those doors everyone sees every day but no one knows where it leads to and no one tries to find out either

---

[16] Laws again. Everwhere was made of human dreams, wishes, fears and whatnot, so nothing a human mind couldn't picture would be able to exist there.

There are similar places, however. There is one full of mice, balls with bells in them and milk that won't make you sick, for instance. And another one that was created from the minds of very large creatures that have all gone extinct; it's a good thing people can't get into either of these.

because it <u>looks</u> locked, one of those doors that has always been there and which does not seem to lead anywhere interesting. No one ever used it; whoever tended the sheep used the gate by the animals' pen and no one seemed to know why this other door was there. No one even cared either, at least not the adults; besides which, people figured, as people tend to do, that it must be locked for a reason, namely to prevent anybody from going through. For the law-abiding people of the town, that was reason enough to stay out.

The door wasn't really locked, of course; that was just a trick the Wardens, once they found out about the door and realised they couldn't destroy it, had used to prevent people from wandering into Everwhere and most likely never coming out. And as to how they came up with the idea, well, Wardens might have no imagination but they know everything about how to trick other people's.

Still, it's strange that no kid ever tried to open the lock or worm her way through it. Sure, kids jumped the fence all the time, trying to get to the sheep and often getting bitten and kicked in the process, but never since it came into existence had any child, or even teenager tried to pick the lock or cut it open. How the Wardens of Everwhere managed to make a locked door completely unappealing to curious children is one of the most mysterious secrets of their trade.

Frank himself could have been caught in their trap, if the door hadn't sprung up in his presence as it had before the Wardens found out about it; fortunately, when he came through he had never bothered to check what the gate was like on this side so he never realized it was locked and never fell for the spell or whatever it was that kept kids from wanting in. Being what he was, all he needed to know was that the door was there and where it led to. The lock was a bit of a puzzle once he saw it, of course, but at close examination it turned out that all he had to do was lift up the chain and open the door, and that was exactly what he did. With a bow and a flourish, he invited his sister to enter his world.

From where she was standing, all Ythoda could see was the same field she had always seen through the fence; the only difference was that the door was open now, instead of closed, but that seemed all. It was a disappointing sight, not what she had been hoping at all, even though she didn't exactly know what that was; still, it didn't look anywhere near like an exciting new game and for a moment, she hesitated if she wouldn't do better to just turn her back and go home instead of following her brother in what could never be anything remotely exciting.

Still, Frank was a very persistent character and, as there was nothing better to do anyway, she eventually did go through the door and in doing so she saw a path.

No grand landscape of breathtaking beauty. No shining city full of fairies or angels of some other mushy thing.

Just a dirt path going into the distance.

Maybe the narrowest, least well-travelled road in Everwhere.

That first path Ythoda walked on in Everwhere brought her straight into her worst nightmare.

But let's not jump ahead too far; Ythoda should get the chance to enjoy Everwhere for a while: it wouldn't be fair otherwise.

Dirt paths aren't very exciting and if Ythoda hadn't been a city girl she might just have shrugged and turned her back on it. But she had spent all her life in a city so a path going off in the distance without any signs of the landscape being inhabited was a very novel experience for her.

Of course, a lot of children would consider "novel" to be a synonym of "scary", but Ythoda had never been one to let her fears get the best of her; besides which, she had Frank to urge her on and to promise her fun adventures, so she set off on the road.

They were walking down a soft slope on a mountain. It was pretty: grassy meadows extended at both sides, specked with flowers of all colours. Some clumps of shrubs broke the view every now and then. The air was mild and the sun warm, but not hot. Frank began to whistle the first bars of "The hills are alive….", but Ythoda punched him into silence- some things are just too much.

7

I t was pretty, but beauty alone won't hold a child's attention for very long.

After they had walked for some time without anything happening, Ythoda began to become bored. And when Ythoda was bored, her imagination would begin running amok and that, which in her own reality was only a source of amusement or annoyance depending on how much sense of humour the audience to her ramblings had, was something that couldn't fail to have an immediate effect on her surroundings in Everwhere. This was something Ythoda herself was unaware about and Frank took so much for granted that the thought of warning her hadn't even crossed his mind.

As we know, Ythoda's imagination had been very much occupied with Andromedans[17] lately, so Frank was not really surprised when some of the brightest coloured flowers amongst the ones that were growing at the edges of the path they were walking on, started spinning and buzzed up into the air, coming to hover before the children. There were a good many flowers, all equally tiny, all gyrating furiously and making a noise like a swarm of bees who buzzed at different pitches to form a strange, almost hypnotic kind of music; as they flew, they moved in front of and around the children, dancing in the air, making strange and beautiful patterns. If Ythoda was startled, it didn't show, maybe because the spectacle was so engrossing as to be almost hypnotic, which could account for the fact that she remained watching their dance with an intent stare for several minutes. And even though Frank was considerably less surprised, he did the same.

---

[17] Cute, little pink ones.

It was very entertaining, but quite dizzying, and Ythoda was beginning to think of swatting them away when the spaceships, for that's what they were, set themselves down on the path and one of them put down a petal to serve as gangway for the leader of the Andromedan space fleet. Before the children's startled eyes, a tiny pink figure descended from the flower-starship holding its hands up in the universal gesture for peace and jabbering something unintelligible in a high-pitched voice the children had to strain their ears to hear, let alone understand.

Even so, any one observing from a safe vantage point, and with foreknowledge of what was going on, would readily have recognized the event as a first contact between our species and the Andromedan Glutnutts[18].

Except in the end the whole thing never happened, because Ythoda, who despite her fascination had been quite a bit more startled than she let on when the ships first took off, was now about to break into a panic and was clearly meaning to stamp the poor aliens into mash. I mean, it's all very well to imagine things, but it's an entirely different kettle of fish to have them come alive before your eyes; and yes, Ythoda had accepted Frank's appearance very calmly, but then again, he was her brother and these were aliens and aliens, no matter how cute, little and pink, are scary because you never know what they want or what they are capable of[19]. So she raised a foot, getting ready to bring it down with all its force upon the poor Andromedan commander and Frank had to hold her back, which wasn't all that easy, as he had been imagined not too strong for his sister to handle.

But he did manage to quiet her and then went on to explain to her that things she imagined came true here. He guessed that those were her

---

[18] Not to be confused with the Andromedan Mondrells, who are eight feet tall, hairy all over, with four arms and long spiky fangs, grumpy, not at all nice and a figment of some sci-fi freak's imagination. Nothing at all like Ythoda's Andromedans, although at a later stage the latter would end up in serious danger of extinction because of the Mondrells, until fortunately these became extinct themselves due to sheer stupidity.

[19] In time, she'd learn that the figments of her imagination existing in Everwhere had exactly the characteristics she had thought them to have, and no others. The only exception was Frank, but that was because, in coming into our world, he had acquired an independence of Ythoda's mind none of its other creatures would ever reach.

Andromedans; she could only confirm, "But I never knew they were <u>that</u> small".

The good news was that she had always imagined them friendly so the chance of Frank and Ythoda getting hurt was almost zero.

As it turned out, the chance of getting to know the aliens was zero too. They were far from aggressive[20] and they had decided to get themselves to safety: the moment they saw Ythoda's foot poised to come down on them they had done a disappearing act (literally; they could, you know).

Which was a pity, because these Glutnutt Andromedans really had a lot to offer to the world: not only did they possess technology humans had only ever dreamed of[21] and a fantastic taste in just about everything, but it also so happened that their society was an example of harmony and peace that would really have....

---

[20] Actually, they were rather wimpy...

[21] Humans in this case meaning Ythoda, to whom the height of technology was a type of sweet that would contain all the vitamins and minerals a growing girl needed and a machine which would allow her to stay up watching forbidden TV programs all night without losing any sleep over it.

…Not appealed to humans at all. Maybe we should just move on now.

Ythoda was very disappointed of course (she might have been even more so if she had known all of the above, but then again, she might have been just as relieved as you and I), but she had to admit she couldn't blame them for not wanting to become Andromedan omelette. So to save herself from disappointment and innocent beings from being mistaken for bugs she decided to be a bit more careful about what she imagined from then on.

8

S o the twins continued their trek.

Time doesn't really work in Everwhere; that's because human minds are really timeless. Time itself is something our bodies have come up with for some reason or another (and even then it doesn't always work as we think it should), and the imagination of a body doesn't reach Everwhere. Anyway, it is good for you know this so you'll understand why Ythoda never thought of it possibly being time to go home[22]

So Frank and she just kept walking and, just before Ythoda got too bored again, they got to a forest.

It was the kind you find in fairy-tales (it actually did belong to some tale or other, but which one it was doesn't matter here), dark and mysterious with a hint of danger; the air was musty but warm, with centenary trees that looked like old, gnarled people, their shadow sides covered in the same soft, fluffy moss that grew all over the ground. There were ferns as tall as a short person, grassy clearings covered in flowers, small animals and birds both hopping and flying about and leaves all over the place. There were all sorts of sounds as well, some easy to identify some not; but underneath it all one could feel a silence of sorts. It was almost as if a part of the forest held its breath in expectation of something that was hidden, something dangerous lurking in the shadows.

You could have expected Little Red Riding Hood to come skipping along on her way to grandma, but, fortunately for Ythoda and

---

[22] Distance does work in Everwhere, but there are ways around that, so I wouldn't worry about how she is to get home if she wanders too far.

Frank, that was not the tale this story belonged to. Not that little girls in Red Riding Hoods are scary or dangerous per-se, though one never knows with these fairy tale characters; wolves, on the other hand, mean trouble wherever they appear, especially if they're hungry for little girls in riding hoods[23].

Ythoda never even gave a thought to what she was missing, not in the last place because Little Red Riding Hood was far from being her favourite tale. In fact, she had never wished herself in any fairy tale at all, which would account its not being the case now.

She did have a wish to see fairies, however. She always had, and now, despite her earlier resolution to be careful with what she wished for, she couldn't resist the temptation.

And, sure enough, they were only a short way into the forest when a little figure came fluttering towards them, tinkling merrily and leaving behind a trail of fairy dust which would help them.....uh.....help them to....yes, fly, that was it....

Ythoda looked at Frank, who shook his head. "That's how you imagine fairies", he whispered.

"Tinkerbell?!".

"Apparently".

"So how do I get to see a real one?"

Ah, now that was a tricky question: you can't see a "real one" of something that doesn't exist. But Frank did give it some thought. "Well, maybe if you just ask for it....you know, like, explicitly or something".

So Ythoda did, and soon almost wished she hadn't, because the forest was suddenly filled with all possible kind of fairy, from sweet little shiny ones with butterfly wings to large, looming creatures that were positively frightening. There

---

[23] Of whatever colour: red, yellow, blue, lime green or even pastel pink, it's all the same to wolves. Not surprising, seeing as they are colour-blind.

were so many of them, all flying about, dancing on leaves or just in the air, playing a jig on a spider web, gossiping with some other fairy, buzzing around the children, twanging thin branches in their faces, pulling their hair, laughing (often at them) and all making so much noise together (this noisiness seems to be the one thing all fairy-imaginers agree on) that one was too overwhelmed to even wish for anything.

So Ythoda did the next best thing: she yelled for silence.

And it worked. All the creatures fell silent; some of them were clearly not too happy about it, especially some of the bigger ones, who

showed it by taking on a rather menacing look, and those ones Ythoda quickly wished away. Then she set about choosing the fairies she would like to get to know better (just at face value, which goes to prove how much we rely on looks- for instance, that dark blue, sulky looking fairy Ythoda discarded would have turned out to be the best stand up comedian ever, if only given the chance) and wished away the rest.

With their number down to a manageable amount and their noise a little above thunder level, which was as quiet as it could possibly get, Ythoda set about to meet and greet the fairies one by one; thinking, and quite rightly so, that a little personal attention would get them to sulk a little less over suddenly having been summoned away from whatever fascinating business they were on. It worked like a charm; fairies are a lot like people, not so much in looks, but because of their egos. In fact, that was the biggest part of most of them, especially the really tiny ones. It took a while, but with Frank's help and using all the charm she could muster, which was not inconsiderable, she at last managed to make friends of the pretty little, or not so little as the case might be, creatures.

And then she asked the fairies for what she thought they would like best, which was a fairy party just like the ones she imagined fairies to have[24]: moonlight, a furry animal orchestra, flowers to dance on, mead to drink, stars coming down to dance as well, getting one's ear pulled by some of the nastier fairies she hadn't spotted on face value. The works.

They had fun.

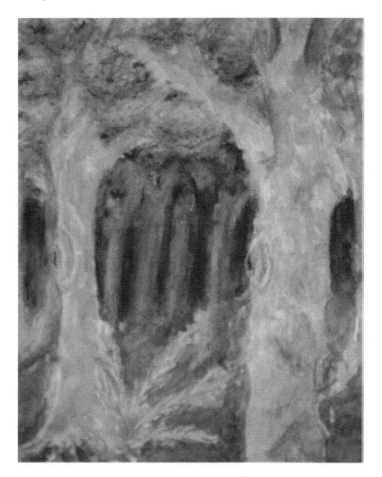

---

[24] And which, from then on and because of Ythoda's imagining, became the way amongst pretty much all kinds of fairies, no matter their culture of origin or their characteristics. And, to be honest, in some fairies' cases, it was a ludicrous thought for them to behave like that; it just didn't fit who they were and never would.

So much for a cultural melting pot.

9

B ut only for a little while, because by then Ythoda was so excited
that she couldn't wait to move on and keep discovering.

She never thought of possible dangers and neither did
Frank, so they moved on blithely, with no other thought than that of
going wherever their feet took them and fully expecting that wherever
that was would prove to be a friendly place with nice people who would
treat them like royalty out of sheer happiness to make their acquaintance.
Except that, if the road they were on was very little travelled on, it was
for a very good reason; it had to be for almost no one to venture
travelling on it. There would have been creatures in Everwhere who
could have warned the children about what was to come, but they never
ran into any.

They probably wouldn't have listened anyway.

So they happily continued on their road and after a while (to be
measured in steps, not hours or even minutes, though, of course, neither
of them bothered counting) they arrived at a village, or something like it.

Frank was puzzled; he had travelled this way more than a few
times and definitely didn't remember any village on the road. Well, the
forest had been new to him too, but that he was used to: woods could
spring up overnight in Everwhere. Villages, however, were a different
thing altogether; after all, a bunch of houses doesn't make a village any
more than one tree makes a forest. And while unmoving things, such as
trees and houses, could indeed spring up overnight, people (of more
kinds than just human) didn't; that is because, while an imagination has
relatively little problem with picturing a landscape in one go, people are
too complicated to come up with more than two or three at a time.

Which meant that villages in Everwhere grew in a very prosaic way: slowly.

Of course, with all the wishing Ythoda had been doing lately, one would expect it to be yet one more of her concoctions, except that it didn't look like anything she might have come up with. The houses, even though their colours were bright, had a gloomy aura, their windows, which were all closed, were dark and dreary; there was no one about and a heavy silence hung in the air. In short, the whole place had an unfriendly feel about it that didn't match Ythoda's normal outlook on the world.

But Frank was never one to pick up on too many subtleties and, unused as he was to danger, he didn't think too much about the whole thing one way or another. And neither did his sister.

On the contrary; they both thought their arriving to the village, whatever it was called, was a serendipitous thing, as both of them were quite hungry by now and this looked like a place where they would find a café or somewhere they could have a bite.

Now, the dangers of this will be obvious to anyone reading this: they were two kids in a village inhabited by a people whose kind they didn't know, they had no idea of the customs of the place, they were two kids alone with nothing and no one to defend them and, most importantly, they had no money on them.

Or rather, Ythoda did (she had just received her allowance the day before), but it was not very likely to be the currency of this place and, whereas the other problems mentioned above might have been solved with cash, the last one dealt directly with the lack thereof.

Risky business.

Frank and Ythoda began walking down the main street; they took it to be that, at any rate, because it was wide and straight and there weren't any other streets, really.

It looked like a potentially beautiful place. The stone-paved street was wide and clean, and all the houses were equally pretty, very picturesque with their bright colours enhancing their quaint architecture. However, it didn't take the children long to realize something was not right, because even with the sun shining straight above them it looked as if the whole street was in shadows. Instead of shining in the sun, all the windows were black, as if, instead of reflecting the light, they were sucking it inwards and making it disappear in their gaping mouths. The street, which should have been flooded with sunshine with only a darker spot where a roof or something else projected onto it, was covered in shadows, which seemed to come creeping from the houses, stealing towards the middle of the street of their own accord like something alive, some dark, malignant entity that wanted to take every bit of light and joy there was left in the world and leave despair in its stead.

It wasn't a pleasant sensation; the children soon began to try to avoid the shadows that kept creeping towards them, sending a chill through their spines every time one so much as brushed by them. It gave them the feeling that something in the place was out to get them and that, despite their cheerful colours, the houses were dark, fearsome places, reaching out to catch them in their gloom.

But worst of all was the emptiness. Nothing moved about on the streets, no people, no animals, not even an insect, and there never was a flicker of movement in any of the houses. Their black windows didn't give any indication as to whether there were living beings in them or not, though it was hard to imagine anyone or anything would be able to survive in them; the exteriors of the houses gave even less away, their windows unadorned with the flowers one would expect in a place like that. Neither were there any trees along the street, even though it was so wide that it could easily have been considered a lane. And then, there was the silence; the whole place was empty of sound, at least not one that was caused by living, breathing, beings. All they could hear was a soft whistling, as that of a wind that could be heard but not felt.

It might have been better for the children to turn back as soon as they began seeing and feeling all of this, but despite their discomfort and their obvious misgivings, they were in too overconfident a state of mind to heed any type of warning now.

Besides, they were hungry.

In a short while (maybe a thousand steps), they arrived to a place where there was some kind of square. It wasn't a friendly little town square like the one the children were accustomed to. On the opposite side from the road they were on stood a large stone edifice with a big wooden door that had a round many-coloured window over it and a steeple with an unmoving weathervane on top; it was a building which they would readily have recognized as a church had it not been surrounded by such an eerie cloud of dark gloom, an atmosphere of sadness so thick that it was almost visible to the naked eye. The square itself was as lifeless as the rest of the town, containing only a dry, dusty fountain and a few crumbling stone benches, with no trees to give shade (not that they would have been needed anyway, with the living shadows creeping from every building and even the fountain), no birds to nest in those nonexistent trees, nothing to give the square even the smallest smattering of pleasantness. The main street continued at the other side, passing between the "church" and the houses that surrounded the rest of the square. Some of these houses had signs outside their doors, old wooden signs, made unreadable with age and swinging creakingly on their hinges like bats hanging from a beam in a bell-tower; it was a fair assumption that they were stores of some kind, and it occurred to Ythoda and Frank that one of them might be just what they were looking for.

Ignoring the fear that had been creeping over them since they entered the village, and which was becoming ever stronger, they went up to one of the houses, whose doors all stood open, and peeked inside.

It was empty; all they could see were some cabinets full of nothing but dust and a counter that was likewise empty; some of the shelves lay broken, there were cracks in the walls and the window pane, an upturned chair lay in one corner and the wooden floor was covered in a thick layer of dust devoid of footprints, not even from a mouse. It had clearly been a store at one time, but no one had bought or sold anything there in a long time. They went on looking.

The next three houses were more or less the same, with some little variations to show that the merchandise had been of a different kind in each of them, such as a big hacking block with a meat cleaver still in it, an old oven with the door lying loose on the floor, or a dais where a customer could stand at a convenient height to have her measurements taken. Strangely enough, however, none of the stores contained any remains of actual merchandise, as if the people who had once kept them had left taking every sellable item with them but for some strange reason leaving behind even the smallest items of furniture, such as stools and rugs.

The fourth house was different. Like most of the other ones, it contained a counter; in this case it was a narrow long one that the children would readily have recognized as a bar had they ever been in one. There were also tables and chairs all around the place, showing that it was, or had been, some kind of inn.

It looked as empty as the rest of the village, but something was different here. For one- though the kids wouldn't remember this until afterwards- it wasn't filled with dust, as were the other houses; also, behind the counter hung a mirror which, in contrast to the one they had seen in another store, was in one piece, and beside it, in two rows of shelves, stood bottles, most of them at some stage of half fullness[25]. Even though there was no one there, it was the only place so far that seemed to have been inhabited and in use very recently indeed. The smell was also different; it wasn't dank and humid, with the cold, mouldy reek of abandoned places but instead had the rather pungent smell of a place full of life and people. Still, though that made a great contrast with the lifelessness all around, it wasn't a pleasant smell: not rank like the reek of unwashed people but more an odour like that exuded by people feeling a strong, negative emotion; there was anguish in it and even fear. This should have been a clear warning for the children, strong enough to make them forget about being hungry for a while and make sure they got out of the place as fast as they could. Unfortunately, there was something else there that made them forget about everything, something that

---

[25] Of course, we could say half emptiness, especially as there is sure to be trouble ahead, but why bother with pessimism when it is an actual fact?

aroused their curiosity and made them slaves to it; because besides the good state of the furnishings and the smell, somehow the inn didn't <u>feel</u> empty. Despite the fact that there weren't any people there, to Ythoda it seemed as if there was a party going on, one she could glimpse from the corner of her eye but which disappeared as soon as she tried to focus on it, only to appear again as soon as she shifted her gaze: a glimpse of a dancing couple here, people raising their glasses in a toast there, children chasing each other across the room...There were sounds as well: snatches of music, voices and laughter that only lasted a moment so that she could hardly even believe she had heard them. Except that, when she asked him about it, it turned out that Frank had perceived them as well.

It might be all but invisible and it might be set in what was possibly the most dreary place in Everwhere, but there definitely was a party going on there and, by the looks of it, they were purposely being left out. And Ythoda hated being left out of anything.

So, even though her fear was now screaming out in alert and Frank looked much less than happy, a budding feeling of anger made Ythoda bold.

She stepped inside, dragging Frank along.

10

There was a party going on all right; at least, there was music, food and drink, and there were people. Definitely people, even by Ythoda's rather cramped human standards[26]. There was a whole crowd of them.

It wasn't a friendly crowd.

Not that any of them threatened the children in any way. In fact, very few spared Ythoda and Frank a glance, and a very fleeting one at that, when the twins entered and stood looking around them in astonishment that grew into dismay. Because, if it was a party, it was the strangest one they had ever seen, one where everybody went about their business completely ignoring everyone else around them. People were eating and drinking, some were even dancing, but they were doing this completely alone. No one talked to anyone else- though some talked alone-, no one smiled, not even privately; they all shied away from each other, shrinking from any kind of contact, with their gazes locked on the ground, their tables or their glasses to avoid looking into anybody else's eyes.

There were all kinds of people, by the looks of them: old and young people, even some children, dressed in every kind of fashion humankind has ever worn, depicted or just imagined, their skins ranging from smooth pitch black to furry milky white, with all the colours of the

---

[26] Which were: two arms, two legs, two eyes, one nose and, of course, one head.

But this, which is thought to be the standard in our world, is only a possibility in Everwhere; there, the number of limbs one has say absolutely nothing about whether one is to be considered people or not. What really counts there is the mind, or maybe the soul; and who is to say that isn't exactly the way it should be?

rainbow and every state of hairiness in between. One could see people with marks of all trades, all walks of life, some clearly rich, some clearly not, most of them somewhere in between, just as in real life. And to top it off, the crowd was composed of members of every more or less intelligent species, such as exist in Everwhere.

On the surface, none of them had anything in common with the rest.

But as she looked at the scene, taking it all in, there was one thing Ythoda could see in each and every face, in every pair of eyes that avoided her own: fear. And it felt as if all those faces, all those eyes, just mirrored the feeling that had been growing in her ever since entering the village; the one that she had been trying to ignore, telling herself there was no reason for it, but which had begun to become ever stronger the moment she set foot in the inn. It was a mounting feeling of fright, one that, despite the eeriness of the place had no discernible origin, as there was no actual danger to be found there, of that Ythoda was sure; the fear just was, forced upon her by some unknown force and slowly, but surely, taking over her will.

She looked round at Frank, and, to her surprise, he too looked fearful. Not only that but, just like everybody else in the inn, he seemed reluctant to meet her eye, to the point where she had to grab him by the shoulders and practically force him to look at her.

"What is it?" she asked.

"I don't know." He was pale. "I'm just so frightened, I don't know why. Aren't you?"

"Yeah, kind of. Come on, let's grab some food and get out of here." But Frank didn't move; he seemed frozen to the ground.

With a mingled feeling of dismay and relief at having something to think of besides her fear, Ythoda realised that she was going to have to take care of him now. That helped her to set aside at least part of her own fright, though she couldn't help but notice that it was growing stronger by the moment and she knew that if they didn't get out soon she too would be unable to escape. She grabbed his hand and together they began to weave their way towards the bar; it wasn't hard, as everybody that stood in the children's way moved from them before they could as much as breathe on them. Ythoda had never in her life seen anybody react in such a way. "What is this place?"

She hadn't realised that she had spoken aloud, but she must have, because there was an answer, almost instantly: "The House of Fear, of course."

She looked around to see whom the voice belonged to. It was difficult to make out any individual in a place as crowded as this, but at last she saw him standing at the top of the stairs, staring down at the crowd, tall and proud as if the all-pervading sense of despair didn't touch him. He stood there with his arms crossed and smile of satisfaction on his lips, an arrogance about his expression as if...as if he thought he owned the place.

He was young, around her age and Frank's, and gorgeous to look at, with his full mouth and straight nose, his dark eyes shining in a tanned face crowned with a shock of fair hair. She almost smiled (almost, but not quite- the fear was still growing) and walked towards him, again dragging Frank with her. This boy seemed the only one not in the grip of fear: maybe he would be able to help them.

But when she got to where he was standing and looked into his eyes, she understood that he was there to do exactly the opposite. Because, as she met his gaze, it was almost as if she were being dragged down into a vortex of darkness, a place where nothing good could be found and from which nothing good could ever spring. And even though she knew she had to get away from him, she just stood there, a few steps lower than the boy, transfixed, looking at him as if he were a serpent and she the bird he had just marked out as his next prey.

Whatever it was that was causing every person in the room to be cowering in fear, this boy was at the centre of it.

He smirked.

11

"Welcome." It was not a friendly greeting, despite the friendly word. "I'm always glad to have new people here".

Ythoda's mouth had gone dry, not so much at the words, ominous though they sounded, but at the cold tone of his voice; she had to swallow hard before she could speak, before she could think of the next thing to say. "Where did you say we were?"

"In the House of Fear." There was a hint of impatience in his voice, as if he didn't like having to explain himself to anyone. "This is my place; it belongs to me. I created it, and everyone here has to abide by my rules," he went on. Again, he smirked.

He was looking her up and down appraisingly, and then did something surprising: he inhaled deeply, as if trying to smell some perfume emanating from her, and then he smiled.

"Oh, yes, you will do." His smile, which she could now see was as cold as his voice, was filled with satisfaction. "Provided you can find it within yourself to follow the rules, of course, but I'm sure even one as brazen as you can learn how to do that eventually." Ythoda didn't want to ask about those rules; at that moment, she didn't want to know anything more about the House of Fear, or the boy or even Everwhere. All she wanted was out.

It took a supreme effort of will to overcome the feeling that was freezing her on the ground, but at last she managed to turn around, away from the boy and his evil, immobilizing stare. She grabbed Frank's hand again and started towards the door.

"There's nowhere to go, you know?" The boy's voice forced her to stop short where the words would only have made her laugh or become angry; that heartless voice, colder than ice, which revelled in her fear and wanted to make her suffer, was now tinged with fury and with lust for revenge, making her know without a shadow of a doubt that something awful would happen to her if she didn't heed it. "Once you come in here, you are nothing, have nothing. Everything you were, everything you owned, everything you felt, it's gone; all you have left is fear. I have a gift, you see, the gift of seeing people's worst fears just by looking into their eyes, and I have made it so that, if you try to escape, that worst fear becomes true as soon as you cross that door. Everyone here knows it; that's why no one dares to leave. Instead, they stay here and try to forget their previous life and suppress their fear. I like that; their being here stops me from being alone…and they feed me with their fear. And now, you will feed me too. I like your fear; it has got a different flavour to it, as if it were mixed with something else, though I can't really make out what it is. It's interesting, though; it makes a nice difference from the others…besides which, I've had them for a long time and they were getting a bit stale. It was high time for a new addition to my collection. Anyway, I suggest you make yourself at home; there are enough rooms and you'll have food and drink in plenty. No one can say I don't take good care of my slaves, just as long as you remember there is no leaving here. There is no way out." He had walked down the few steps that separated him from his new guests and had taken Ythoda's chin in his hand with a proprietary air, looking straight into her eyes. His gaze engulfed her, drew her soul to him, kicking and screaming and trying uselessly to release itself from the dark light of those stony eyes. She felt as if she were disappearing, drowning in the blackness of his soul; she could feel herself shrinking, becoming the nothing he had told her she was, sinking deeper and deeper in that cold, black void. She was about to faint and would have fallen to the ground if he hadn't released her. It couldn't have been more than a few minutes, but it seemed like an eternity to her as she stood there, swaying, disoriented, her head still reeling from her voyage into hell.

She recovered her balance and stood stock-still. She seemed paralysed.

Now it was Frank's turn to grab her hand and drag her away, not just because she was scared, but because he could feel she was beginning to become angry as well. It was her anger that the boy could taste in her fear, though neither he nor she knew it.

But Frank did; he knew all the power of Ythoda's anger, even though he had never felt it himself. It was her greatest weapon against any problem, as it made her want to rush headlong into it and solve it, no matter what the cost to her or who else got hurt in the process; nothing else existed when Ythoda got angry.

And her anger was the strongest when she wasn't in control.

It was just that here, there was no option but to release control, and Frank knew that, or at least thought he did. This boy, whoever he was in the real world [27], was clearly much too powerful to handle here, even for Ythoda in full blaze; and she wasn't even in half blaze now. The only thing for it now was to submit to the situation and try to make the best of it, though even Frank knew full well that there was no possible "best" about their situation..

So he grabbed her hand and pulled her towards a table, one where there was food. They sat down, and gloomily ate, and then drank, not even knowing what it was they were eating, not even perceiving the taste of the food, even though it probably was good stuff. It didn't matter; nothing matters when your life seems over.

Their hunger was satisfied soon enough, their thirst quenched, and they should have been feeling much better. And in a way, they were feeling better now that their physical discomfort was gone. But there remained that dull aching in the pits of their stomachs that usually comes with the foreboding of something bad about to happen to you.

And bad things were lurking indeed, just behind the door. Frank knew it and Ythoda knew it, even though they wouldn't be able to say what those awful things were should anybody have asked; all they knew was that "outside" had suddenly become a dangerous, even deadly, place to be and even though the House of Fear was an evil place as well, both knew there was nothing they could do about it. They were trapped, forced to feel a continuous fear they couldn't fight because the danger out there was too great to face. The feeling weighed them down, made them heavy and listless, all the more so because they knew there was no escaping it, that they were condemned to keep feeling it for the rest of their lives. And there was that other feeling too, which made it increasingly harder to look each other in the eyes.

---

[27] "Real" people don't usually go into Everwhere, but they do have alter egos there. An alter ego is an image you create of yourself, something you would like to be but are not (or maybe not completely). Our alter egos live in Everwhere, just like imaginary friends and brothers do.

The feeling was shame.

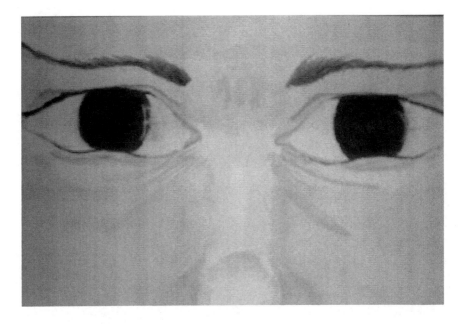

12

Fear is really an instinctive reaction to danger. It makes our senses keener and our body alert, ready to flee at a blink.

Fear is a very useful emotion if one is living in a world full of dangers of every kind, a world where there is hardly any shelter from the elements and one bolt of lightning can set fire to the whole of your surroundings, a world where your only weapons against the countless predators' fangs and claws are your hands, a stick or a stone. Fear was needed in that world, the primitive world of our ancestors, to whom every natural phenomenon was a god; and with gods, you never know whether they're out to help you or kill you.

Fear is a powerful sensation too, and it can even be pleasant. So much so that people look for ways to make themselves feel it on purpose. Some people even go as far as looking for it in situations of real danger; most of us don't go that far, because allowing yourself to be frightened on purpose is one thing, getting yourself into danger quite another. Most people don't consider that a very smart thing to do. But all of us have at some time or another wanted to experience the thrill of a dangerous situation, of the adrenaline rushing through our bodies, which makes us feel that we have suddenly developed superhuman strength or speed. In some instances, fear can actually provide us with courage and spur us on to action.

But there can be shame in fear too. Children are taught very young that there is nothing to be afraid of in their rooms at night because, after all, imaginary things can't hurt you; and even if, deep down, we all feel that's not true, we have chosen to believe it because otherwise the world would be too fearful a place to live in.

But true or not, children are taught to be ashamed of their fear. They are told to stop imagining things, that they are too old to believe in monsters that live under their beds; they learn that to need a light in their rooms at night is a sign of weakness and that being weak is the worst thing that can happen to them.

We can allow ourselves to be frightened on purpose; we can- with some trouble- forgive ourselves for being afraid in a physically dangerous situation. But the fears we have of things that are out of our knowledge and out of our control, those we try to hide even from ourselves.

And we feel weak and worthless if we allow ourselves to fear.

The shame was even worse than the fear in the House. You could see it in the way people slunk past each other, not so much afraid of what the other one could do (after all, they were all in the same situation and hurting each other was more likely to make it worse than to make it better) but of someone looking in their eyes and seeing the weakness there.

So people's fear made them ashamed, and their shame made them want to avoid each other and that, in turn, made the fear grow stronger because, even if deep down you know they won't, the people you don't look at are the most likely to hurt you. Because when you don't see something, or someone, you have no control, no way of knowing whether or when they will attack you, making them the things you fear the most.

And there was no way out of the vicious circle.

No way at all.

Just the door.

13

Ythoda was watching the door in a way that Frank knew very well, her eyes shining with the fire of action. It was the look she had when she was up to something and this time it made Frank uneasy. The idea of his sister trying something made him cringe, and that was strange, because there was no reason whatsoever for him to feel that way.

Fear was a novel sensation for Frank, as he had never really feared anything. He hadn't even known danger since he came into existence.

His games with Ythoda had always been of the safe kind, even when high up in a tree or fighting with the boys next door. Because Frank didn't have an actual body in the "real" world, he had never even felt any pain, let alone gotten a scratch or a bruise; and because they were in Ythoda's world, instead of his native Everwhere, the make-believe games they were both so fond of and which could have caused him some harm at home became completely safe here. Besides which, he didn't have, and had never had any enemies and had never needed to worry about any kind of predator. Frank had always been perfectly safe, protected from harm by his sister's fond imagination. If anybody had a reason to be fearless, it was he.

It was very strange then, that he should be feeling so afraid when there was absolutely no cause for him to be; after all, the Fearmaster wouldn't have been able to "see" his worst fear, simply because there was none. But, apparently, the boy did have the capacity to cause fear to appear in his subjects, senseless, meaningless fear without reason or rhyme.

If Frank had ever given any thought to the concept of fear and the reason he had none, he might have realised much sooner why the

Fearmaster couldn't possibly have any hold on him; he would then have known that he, at least, was free. As it was, the thought didn't dawn on him until he saw his sister getting herself in battle mode.

The children had been sitting at the table for quite a while now, doing nothing. They didn't look around them, their normal curiosity forgotten in their predicament; they didn't invent any games, they didn't speak, seeing as they couldn't find anything to speak about. They didn't even feel the need to move. All they could do was sit there and feel miserable and try very, very hard not to avoid each other's face; they both knew that if they allowed that to happen, then they would really be caught forever in what made the House of Fear a prison no one ever escaped from.

The twins fought the shame, because they couldn't fight the fear. Still, it was becoming ever more difficult not to give in and not to give up.

But now, Ythoda was sitting straight and still, her gaze fixed on the door.

Her eyes seemed made of stone; her face was an expressionless mask. There was nothing about her to suggest what she was thinking or, for that matter that she was even thinking at all.

Yet Frank knew better, because when his sister looked like that, it was because she was about to explode into a frenzy of action; he also knew that she would do whatever it was she set out to do regardless of who stood in her way. Seeing that brought Frank to his senses, making him realize that there was no danger, could be no danger at all waiting for him behind the door of the House. He could just get up and leave and none of his fears would come true because there weren't any. He also suddenly understood that, whatever Ythoda was planning, it was very unlikely that she would really carry it out: if he had been in the grip of a senseless, baseless fear that had been keeping him from walking out, how could she beat a fear that probably did have a base, even if she had never discussed it with him?[28]

---

[28] In fact, she had never discussed any fear with him; after all, no girl in her right mind would voluntarily give any brother the slightest weapon against her, imaginary twin or not.

It was a heartbreaking thought, his sister getting so revved up for action and then not being able to go through with it. Frank knew he couldn't face her devastation when the anger subsided and she realised she had let her fear win for the first time in her life, so he decided it was up to him to get them both to freedom. No matter what his sister had to face, it would be less dangerous in the long run than staying in the House of Fear. He looked Ythoda in the eye; even if she looked as though she didn't even see him, he knew she would register it. "I'm out of here," he announced. "Are you coming?"

He got up and walked to the door. Ythoda was beside him in a blink.

As he reached for the door handle, a hand grabbed his own, preventing him from opening it.

Frank turned slowly, knowing full well who it would be; it was the boy, the Fearmaster. "You can't go out. It's dangerous out there. You'll get hurt." The voice didn't convey any concern for Frank's wellbeing; it only projected anger at the possibility of anyone escaping his control. The eyes boring into Frank's were darker than ever, piercing, controlling, evil, full of hatred towards this boy who dared stand up to his power. But Frank wouldn't be fazed any more; he looked straight into those eyes and saw nothing there for him to fear.

He laughed. "We'll see about that".

He grabbed the door handle and turned it. The hand around his wrist turned to stone. "I told you, you couldn't go out!"

"I'll go wherever I please!" Frank jerked his hand free and, turning around, pushed the Fearmaster away from him angrily; the Fearmaster staggered, recovered and threw himself at his opponent, trying to grab at his throat. Frank evaded him narrowly and, with his left hand, threw a punch, which hit empty air.

If possible, the inn went more silent than ever when the two boys took hold of each other, toppling over and grappling on the ground. All there was to see for what seemed an eternity was a tangled mass of

Still, Frank wasn't a fool and years of sharing Ythoda's world had taught him a thing or two about being afraid, albeit only theoretically. In the process, he had also picked up on some of his sister's demons; but he had too much sense to let on.

And he loved her too much, too.

flailing limbs; all that could be heard was the angry hissing of the fighters and the sound of flesh hitting flesh.

Suddenly, Frank emerged, his nose bloodied, one eye black, sitting on top of his opponent's chest. He grabbed the boy's shirt and dragged him upright, then pushed him away again.

"I will go now. And so will my sister."

The silence was leaden; the whole inn held its breath at Frank's daring. No one had ever defied the Fearmaster like that,; no one had ever tried to escape in full sight. And those who had fled had always, without fail and in plain view of all, encountered their own worst, most dangerous fears… and now, a mere kid had done what no one had ever dreamed of before. He had beaten the Fearmaster, who now stood with a blackened cheek and ruffled clothes, glaring. Was there a hint of insecurity in his gaze?

Suddenly, the Fearmaster laughed, a hollow, joyless laugh. "I have no option but to let you go, but she can't come with you." The voice was cold with anger, but there was also a gloating in it that made Frank shudder.

But he made himself stay calm and continue to unblinkingly face the Fearmaster. "And why not? There isn't any danger here. There is nothing in this land that will hurt either of us."

"Perhaps that's true for you; I knew right away that there was something not right about you, but I guess I misjudged you in thinking that you did have fears, even if they were incredibly well hidden, and that I would find them eventually. You truly don't have any fears. But she does, your sister, and one of them, the worst one, will come true if she leaves this place; for as soon as you come in, that is where the way out leads you to: your worst nightmare. Will you really lead her into danger?"

"Better in danger out here than in there with you. Ythoda, are you coming?"

Frank turned around and started to walk. He was so sure that Ythoda would follow that he didn't bother to check.

The look in her eyes had told him enough.

He had only walked a few steps when his sister flashed past him.

They were clear.

14

"Thanks for getting me out of there. I don't think I would have found the nerve if you hadn't started first. Man, you were great! I never knew you were able to fight like that!"

Ythoda stopped in the middle of the square and turned towards her brother.

Frank wasn't there.

Ythoda looked around, but he was nowhere to be seen. She was annoyed; he might just have saved her from the House of Fear and for that she would forever be grateful, but surely this was no time for hide and seek! They had to get out of the village and preferably out of Everwhere as soon as they could, and Frank should know that. Imaginary or not, her brother was more than smart enough to realise that as long as she stayed in the Land, she would be susceptible to the Fearmaster carrying out his threat to her. And if the door they had gone through was indeed the only exit from the place, they were going to need lots of eyes if they wanted to arrive there unscathed; she couldn't remember how long it had taken her to get to Fear Town- for some reason[29] her watch had stopped working the moment they went through the door; she did know, however, that it had been a long walk. Very long. Too long...

She swallowed hard, remembering the look in the boy's eyes, his cold, cruel voice and knowing in the bottom of her soul that he would never give up until he had caught and punished her, especially now that he had been humiliated before the eyes of all those poor people inside

---

[29] Like, time not existing in Everwhere. Which would have been obvious had she known that, except it was one more of the things Frank had neglected to mention to her.

"his" House first by being lured into a fight[30] and afterwards by being beaten.

But there was nothing to be done about it. Her brother had gone and concealed himself somewhere and she was going to have to search for him in all possible places, probable or not. She could call out for him, but that wouldn't do any good; if Frank decided to play hide and seek, he would do it the right way: without any noise. And he was good at it too.

She sighed. And began to look for places he could have hidden.

She was quite sure he wouldn't venture into any of the empty houses; after what had just happened to them in the inn, he wouldn't be about to risk any more weirdness for either of them, no matter how lifeless a house looked and felt; you just never knew. Besides, dust always made him sneeze.

So she looked for nooks and crannies, corners of things, jutting walls a boy could squeeze behind, under, or into in order to hide. Like behind a statue or a fountain. Or under a bench. Or...

The problem was, there weren't many such places in the village. There was the dry, dusty old fountain in the middle of the square. It was empty of water and proved to be equally empty of Frank. Some stone benches in what should have been the sunny side of the square looked inviting enough to squat behind. Still no Frank. And as those were pretty much the only options for hiding in the square, she looked around a few corners, but no one said "boo".

Ythoda was not amused. She was beginning to lose her patience. And there was this peculiar, cold feeling in the pit of her stomach again, a feeling she didn't welcome at all.

And then, sudden relief.

The door of a house across the square, the only one the children hadn't looked in before, stood ajar, strangely welcoming in all the

---

[30] A fight he probably had known full well he would lose. People like The Fearmaster hardly ever rely on physical violence but this, which in most others would be proof of a peaceful disposition, in them is sheer cowardice: they don't refrain from hitting others because they don't want to hurt them, but because they don't want to get hurt themselves.

gloominess around it. Through the crack, she could see a light shining merrily, trying to and succeeding in dissipating the shadow that crept from under the house. The light, the fact that the Fear Shade couldn't overcome it, everything suggested that behind that door didn't lay an empty house.

For a moment, Ythoda wondered how it could be that they hadn't noticed it before, but the thought vanished without a trace before she could even question the fact.

Because she could see that the light was actually sunshine. And she could hear noises coming from the other side as well, noises of children playing. She knew at once that Frank would be there, and that he would be safe. She relished the thought of yelling at him for not telling her where he was going and, most of all, she felt great relief at finding what could only be a safe place so fast, so easily. Almost too easily...

Ythoda shook the thought away and crossed the square at a trot.

She pushed the door open. Her hand held not a heavy wooden door but a tattered wooden gate that everyone thought was locked.

Ythoda smiled and stepped through the doorway.

She was home.

15

The park was flooded with sunshine, just as it had been when they left.

Everything else also looked in place; there even were exactly the same people sitting on the benches as there had been before, and the woman with the stroller hadn't quite finished passing by the door yet.

That threw Ythoda, who had expected it to be at least the middle of the night, if not the next day. After all, they had been away for ages, or so it felt like to her. But after giving some consideration to what her senses told her, she realised soon enough that time must pass differently, or rather not at all, in Everwhere. The thought tickled her because it meant that if she went back (and despite the House of Fear, now she was safely home in her own town, out of the Fearmaster's reach, she saw no reason not to), she and Frank would be able to spend as much time as they wished exploring it and no one would ever be the wiser. Quite a change from their normal imaginary adventures under time constraint!

Frank still wasn't to be seen, however, which was a little strange; one would expect that, after fighting a boy for her and getting a black eye out of it- his first one ever, by the way- he would be waiting for her at the gate, not only to make sure she was really safe but to reap some praise…well, a lot of praise, as well. But on the other hand, he did have a habit of acting before thinking so it wasn't all that surprising that he hadn't waited for his sister. He must have assumed that she would have the sense to find the door back into town and that once she was in the park, she'd know where he was.

She did, too; it was quite obvious after all: he had taken her to Everwhere because she couldn't think of a game and now it was her turn again. Plus that he must be convinced that all she had seen would give enough wings to her imagination to keep living on their desert island for quite a while longer. So she went there to look for him.

Smiling, she pushed through the bushes that protected their "desert island" from view. It was really a small clearing in a ring of bushes, standing a bit back from one of the smaller paths that crisscrossed the park and, since few people walked there and even fewer would be likely to get it in their heads to go and see what those bushes were all about, it

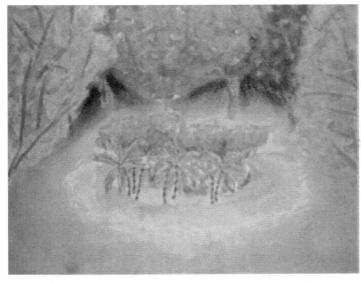

was the perfect place to play and never be noticed or disturbed.

Frank loved this hideout of theirs and he sometimes went there just to think, when they had had an argument or when Ythoda was too busy with homework, or simply because he had something he was wondering about. Ythoda herself did too, but far less often- she was more of a doer than a thinker, after all, and besides, she was the type of child who liked being around people all the time, the more the merrier.

All in all, she was so sure that she'd find him there that she began talking to him even before she had made it all the way through the bushes. "You know, that's a great place you've taken me to. I'd love to see more of it and…" She stopped in mid-sentence, not because she didn't know what to say next but because there was no one to say it to. Frank wasn't there.

It wasn't at all like Frank not to be there. Ever since he had come to her, Ythoda had never been alone, not really.

Oh, yes, Frank did like to withdraw for a while at times, but he always told her where he would be, just in case she needed him. And besides, he was always back before she had time to miss him.

Frank was always there, with her and for her, no matter what. And he would never have done anything that looked even remotely like abandoning her.

Never until now.

Ythoda sat down on the grass of the island, too stunned at this completely unexpected turn of events to know what to do next; indeed, she didn't even know what to think. Questions were racing through her mind, too fast and too many of them to make any sense of, let alone come up with any kind of answer to.

Could it be that Frank hadn't made it out of Everwhere after all? Had he somehow missed the door, even though it was the only place he could possibly have gone to? Or was it? Had she not looked for him well enough, was she the one who, in her haste to get away and her joy at seeing some actual light, had left him? Had something else than the Fearmaster, possibly even something worse, prevented him from leaving? Was he still out (or in) there, waiting for her to come and save him this time? Or had he simply decided that it was time for him to go out on his own again? Had she done something to push him away? Was he angry with her? Or…

There was that cold feeling again, the one she had hoped never to feel again.

Ythoda decided not to feel it again; instead, she shook her fear off. "He has gone home", she decided.

She would do the same.

16

It wasn't far from the park to Ythoda's house, only a couple of blocks. And, since she had been living in the same house all her life, and had been coming to the park by pretty much the same route at least every other day for years, it was not surprising that she knew, at least by sight, most of the people who lived in the houses or worked in the stores along the road. It was the people and not the buildings who, to her, made the place: their voices, their interactions, knowing which people were on speaking terms with each other and which didn't even greet, some of their more conspicuous habits; all those things we don't often pay much attention to but that nevertheless are an integral part of what makes our lives "our" lives.

On the other hand, people are easy to overlook, especially those you see every day, and often we don't realize someone is missing until we for some reason need them to be there. It's not that we don't care about the, shall we call them, "fringe" people in our lives, meaning, those who are part of our daily routine without belonging to our family or close friends; it's just that we are so used to seeing them in their place that we assume they are there even if they're actually not.

That is probably why it took Ythoda a few streets to realize that she wasn't greeting or being greeted by anyone she knew.

That wasn't normal; usually she couldn't get through a street without exchanging at least two or three greetings: with the lady from the bookstore where she spent a good deal of her pocket money and who, in return, kept back copies of her favourite authors' new books for her, to make sure she wouldn't miss out; with the baker's little boy who always played on the sidewalk in front of the shop and loved to show her his toys, and also the baker himself; with the Italian ice-cream man at his usual corner; or with a few of her schoolmates, though not any of her best friends- those lived further away…

When she first noticed it, she thought that maybe it was only because she had been so distracted by her search for Frank that she had just ignored everyone else. But a closer examination of her recollections of the last few minutes proved that it was more than just not exchanging greetings: she couldn't remember seeing any of them, not even dimly. It was a strange thing to experience, too strange to ignore, so, despite her hurry, she stopped and took a good look at her surroundings to make sure she wouldn't miss any more of her acquaintances.

None of them were there.

The buildings were still there, the shops all accounted for; she made quite sure of that. Everything was just as it had been that morning, only a few hours before; the houses were in the right places and had the right colours, down to the flowers on the window-sills, and she could have sworn everything else was still in place: lampposts, the benches some of the neighbours had put next to their front doors so they could sit outside of an evening, the mailbox on the corner…Even the shops hadn't changed at all; the butcher's still had the notch in the door from the time she had kicked it open in a temper (which had been entirely her mother's fault, so Ythoda refused to feel guilty).

It was just the people: there were enough of them out and about, but not one of them was someone she had seen the day before, or that very morning. None of the usual benches was occupied, though an elderly man was reading a newspaper on the bench outside number 17, the house that was inhabited by two sisters and their cats; they did at times sit outside, but never at that hour, and Ythoda was sure she had never seen the man. Also the woman shaking a blanket out of the second floor window in number 24 was unfamiliar to her, as was everybody else. Even the salespeople in the shops were different, all of them, which made no sense as most businesses on that street, were family owned. And even in the unlikely event that every shopkeeper had decided to hire new personnel, it was next to impossible they would have done so at the same time, let alone in the few hours between that morning and now.

It was very odd.

Odd, and unsettling.

All those people Ythoda knew or at least recognised, where were they? There were too many for all of them to have disappeared, especially in so short a time. It was too strange to ignore, but also too strange to believe, and Ythoda didn't quite know which stand to take.

Was someone, somehow for some weird reason playing a complicated trick on her? She was well aware of the fact that she had a few enemies, some of whom would take every possible opportunity to do her a bad turn[31], but it would have been impossible for any of them to pull such a stunt.

Unless...

There was that cold feeling again.

Ythoda began walking faster; her haste to get home and find Frank was now complemented by a need to see, to greet someone familiar, even if it was someone she disliked. At this moment, she didn't care who it was, as long as she knew her face, or his as the case may be; she would have been overjoyed to see even her worst enemy, provided she saw her and reacted to her, no matter how nastily. After all, she could always pay her back later, when she knew everything was as it should be, when she had lost that feeling...

She turned a well-known corner, her heart racing half in expectation half in fear of disappointment, and then heaved a sigh of relief; there on the pavement, in front of the bakery, just as it should be, a little boy was playing with...

A doll?

In all the years she had stopped to admire the child's toys and pat his head before moving on, she had never seen him with anything other than "real boy's toys" in his hands[32]. So...since when did the baker have a little daughter?

_____

[31] Just as she never had any qualms about returning the favour, if possible with interest.

[32] Just as Ythoda's parents and most others in town, the little boy's mother and, especially, father, had very fixed ideas about which activities were appropriate for a child of which gender. A boy playing with a doll would hardly fit any of those standards.

Of course, many little boys managed to circumvent these expectations by "stealing" their sister's dolls and, for instance, carry out scientific experiments on them or testing

The girl had stopped playing, her small body stiff and unmoving, and was looking at Ythoda, who had called out a greeting as she turned the corner. Even from that distance, she could see that the look on the little one's face was not the open, excited, friendly expression of a child being approached by someone she knows and trusts. And, when Ythoda reached her and smilingly complimented her on her pretty doll, the child averted her eyes, her dark, curly head shying away from Ythoda's hand, which was half-raised as if to pat her hair.

The cold feeling that had been nestling in her stomach and that she had tried so hard to ignore began to spread: in the fleeting second before the little girl turned her face away, Ythoda had been able to see an expression that shook her, because she recognised, or thought she recognised the look in the child's eyes; the eyes were dark with distrust and fear and filled with shame at the same time. Never in her whole life had she seen an expression like that in such a young one, not in her town, not in her life, except in one place: impossible as it seemed, she was sure it was the same as everyone wore in the House of Fear.

Was it possible that the Fearmaster had somehow...?

No! No! NO!

Ythoda tried to shake off the thought, but she found herself shaking instead.

Panic was invading her.

She needed to go home.

She needed her mother.

Ythoda began to run.

---

whether they had superpowers. And, since usually the dolls didn't come out of it unscathed, their parents' scoldings were tinged with relief: boys will be boys, after all.

17

Her house was still there, the windows open as usual, to let fresh air in while her mother cleaned the bedrooms. The doormat still spelled "Welcome" in faded red letters on a green background and a few of the shells along the path to the front door were still missing from when Frank and she had decided to play "a day at the beach."

As she stopped for a minute to catch her breath, Ythoda felt a wave of relief flooding over her.

Home was still there, and she knew that nothing bad could ever happen at home. There, in her own place, with her own family, in the centre of her world she would be safe from any danger and from any nightmare.

No one could reach her there, no matter how hard they tried. Her parents might not be all she would like them to be, they might not always understand her as she would like to be understood, but she knew for a fact that they loved her no matter what.

And they would never let anything bad happen to her.

She rushed through the garden fence, over the path to the back door, and stormed into the house.

She didn't wipe her feet, she slammed the door, she shouted for her mother, she shouted for Frank.

She completely forgot her manners.

She didn't care if her mother yelled at her; she <u>wanted</u> her mother to yell at her. She wanted to feel that everything was as it should be, that, here at least, everything and everybody was in their place.

There was no reaction.

Ythoda stood in the hall, dumbfounded. An entrance like the one she had just performed had always been a sure way to attract her very manner-conscious mother's attention and today's storming of the house had been a prime example of Ythoda's capacity for stampede, but she had been met with dead silence. Not only did her mother not come rushing out of wherever she was to scold her noisy daughter, but also Ythoda couldn't hear her anywhere in the house. That in itself was very strange; her mum was always busy and it wasn't often that her activities didn't carry some sound with them, whether it was the din of the vacuum cleaner or the jingling of dishes being washed.

The absence of sound created a strange atmosphere in the house; from where she was standing, Ythoda could see a good way up the stairs and into both the kitchen and the living room. Nothing looked any different from the ordinary but somehow there hung an emptiness in the house that made the well-known rooms and furniture seem heavy and even hostile.

The cold feeling extended a little further…

Angrily, Ythoda shook the feeling away, or tried to.

She must stop being such a baby! She was home now, wasn't she? Home, where she was safe?

Everything was OK, she was sure of it; the odd feeling in her stomach, the weight of the house around her, they were no more than silly fancies she had to stop feeding right now!

Determined to prove it to herself, Ythoda resolved to walk around the house and show her eyes that everything was in perfect, normal order. The kitchen, for starters, was all right. Mum had cleaned up the remains of their breakfast as usual, the dishes had been washed and put away, and everything else was where it was supposed to be. There wasn't even a crumble on the table (there never was); mum's apron was hanging on its usual hook on the door and the tea towels matched perfectly. It was the epitome of kitchen, perfection made kitchen; it was her home's kitchen.

Except that at this time of day her mother usually had just had a cup of coffee, and Ythoda couldn't smell it…

She went on, quickly, not choosing to ponder the matter any further.

The living room was messier; though all the furniture was in perfect array and had clearly been dusted only a little while ago, Ythoda's drawing block and coloured pencils were still lying on the table where she had left them, even though her mother had told her to put them away before she went to play in the park. "I guess Mum's finally gotten tired of picking up after me." Ythoda told herself it was about time too, though in her heart she knew full well that was just an excuse she was making, a reason she was giving herself for ignoring the coldness which had crept up just a tiny bit further.

She went to the stairs, listened, or rather hoped, for sounds of housework: a vacuum cleaner, the washing machine, windows being opened or closed, anything that would suggest her mother was upstairs. There was nothing, no footsteps, no shuffling, not even the sound of breathing.

How could that be, though? Surely, there must be someone there; where else could Mum be otherwise? And where was Frank, for that matter? He should have been home ages ago, so why didn't he come down as soon as she got home?

She went up the stairs, checked her parent's bedroom, the bathroom, her own bedroom.

Nobody.

The cold feeling was beginning to become stronger, harder to ignore. She decided Mum must be out doing the shopping and that Frank was probably in the attic playing with their Legos.

The attic was empty. The castle they had started building together two days before was still untouched- and unfinished, even though Frank had been very keen on getting it done; it had been a great point of contention and they had been arguing about it the day before because Ythoda had suddenly become bored with it while Frank was still in full steam, suggesting all kinds of new features they had never tried before. But Ythoda had refused to continue working on it with the excuse that it was silly, a stupid, childish game for stupid little kids, which Frank naturally had felt to be very offensive[33]. Maybe that was why...

Ythoda's stomach clenched.

NO!

Frank had gone to the shop with Mum, although she couldn't see him, of course. Despite that, Frank liked to go with her sometimes, just as he liked helping her with the household work. Not that she noticed of course, because the only mess he could pick up was his own imaginary one; still, doing things like that for her made him feel she was his mother too even if she didn't even know it herself, and that he was showing her how much he loved her, even if she couldn't return his love.

Yes, that was why he wasn't there, why he wasn't waiting for her, to reassure her and to discuss their adventure with her. He was just doing something he had always loved to do and had momentarily forgotten about everything else; that happened, there was nothing strange about it, it was all very normal, very, very, normal...there was no reason for her hands to shake like this, or for her to feel so cold. There was nothing wrong, nothing could be wrong, everything was just fine. After all, she was home now, the Fearmaster...
NO!

Ythoda forced herself to stay calm, to walk down the stairs rather than run, to pretend breathing wasn't becoming more difficult every minute, to ignore her heart trying to break free from her chest.

She walked into the kitchen, managed to fill the kettle and put it on the stove to make herself a nice cup of tea; it was what Mum always did when someone was upset, and it usually helped too.

She ignored the puddle by the sink, caused by her spilling more water than went into the kettle; her mother would have shouted at her to mop it up straight away, but she couldn't bother about that. The only important thing now was to get that cup of tea, the cup of comfort she always got when she came home in tears because of an argument with a friend or because some other kid had insulted her. The water didn't take too long to boil, mainly because she had put hot water from the tap in

---

[33] "Childish" is a hateful word to have flung at one when you are beginning to grow up; imaginary kids are no exception to that.

the kettle, completely against her mother's teachings, but Ythoda had no time for niceties now; she needed to sit down with that cup as soon as possible because when she did, it would mean that everything around her was normal. Ythoda needed life to feel normal, so she ignored anything that didn't fit with the ordinary course of matters: spilled water, warm water, they didn't belong and must be overlooked.

She poured the water in the mug, put a teabag in, opened the larder cupboard and took out the forbidden tin...

Of course Mum was off to the shop! There were no biscuits in the house!

But Ythoda had already seen her mother's red shopping bag, the one she always took when she went to buy groceries standing in the corner beside the fridge. Of course, she could have forgotten it in her haste to go and buy her daughter's favourite biscuits...

Except that on the living room table, next to her paper and her pencils, lay her mother's black purse, her every day one where she kept her money, her keys, her agenda and a pen, paper tissues, a little-used lipstick, a pocket mirror, a comb...

Going through the list of the odds and ends in Mum's purse didn't make her feel better. Far from distracting her from the truth, it brought reality even closer because she knew full well that the one thing her mother would never forget, no matter how big the hurry she was in, was her purse; that had never happened as long as Ythoda had lived. It hadn't even happened that day when Dad had had his accident and they had rushed off to the hospital in a hurry only to find that he had just sprained his wrist; there could be no reason for it to happen now, unless...

The cold feeling she had been refusing to call fear had now spread through her whole body; it was screaming in every one of her nerves, it was forcing a way through her chest and her throat and into her mouth.

It was trying to get her to give in to itself, to acknowledge it had a good reason to be there, that the thing she had feared the most had actually come true.

She pressed her lips tight together, not wanting to let fear win yet.

It couldn't be that, it couldn't be what she was thinking…imagining. It was all in her head, there was a perfectly reasonable explanation for all of this and she was overreacting because the F…that boy had frightened her more than she wanted to admit. Well, he had been scary, but he wasn't here, he didn't have any power here, couldn't have any power over her life.

Ok, there must be some unusual situation for her mother not to be there and not to have brought…but that didn't mean that…There had to be someone who knew what was going on, someone who would be waiting for her to come so they could explain it to her and take her to her mother. All Ythoda had to do was find them and ask. Just ask, and everything would be all right…

18

Next door, someone was working in the garden, pruning the hedge crookedly with the same big shears she had so often seen her neighbour use on his perfectly shaped plants; he was a young man, dressed in some kind of gardening outfit, with patches on the knees of his trousers and a straw hat included, but his actions were clumsy and uncoordinated, not at all like those of a real gardener. It seemed a miracle indeed that he hadn't yet injured himself with those great scissors.

It hardly came as a surprise to Ythoda that she didn't know him at all.

Her heart did sink, though; she really had hoped the joke, or whatever it was, wouldn't go as far as this. Her family might not be there- she forced herself to think "right now", because they couldn't be far away, they couldn't have just disappeared - and she really hadn't seen anyone she recognized since coming out of Everwhere, but there had to be someone left, someone she could talk to and ask about her parents. No matter how much they hated her and now unhappy they wanted to make her, even the most ferocious enemy must realise that, in order to keep her sanity, she really needed a friendly face at this time.

It didn't look as if the man's face would turn out to be a friendly one, however. In fact, the expression on his face looked suspiciously similar to that of the little girl in front of the baker's shop.

Suspiciously similar to that of the "guests" in…Ythoda put her hands over her ears, as if by doing that she could prevent herself from thinking the name of the place.

His expression, or rather, the feeling of unease it awoke in her, didn't make it easy for Ythoda to approach him, or even want to, but she knew she had to. She needed to speak to someone, anyone who might have an inkling of what might be going on; she must ask for an explanation, maybe get some information that would help her make sense of what was happening- if there were any sense in it. Despite her trying to convince herself of the contrary, Ythoda was seriously beginning to doubt that there was.

"Excuse me, Sir?" Nothing.

"Sir?" Again, no answer, though her new neighbour began to shift uncomfortably at her persistence.

"Please, sir, I really need to ask you...?"

"Yes?" Finally, he gave an answer, though only in a whisper, barely audible. Also, she noticed the man wasn't looking at her directly; he kept his face half averted and glanced at her sideways from under his eyelashes. Clearly, he was avoiding her face, just as she had- without realising it- been expecting ever since she met the baker's new little daughter.

She asked him about her old neighbours. Reluctantly, like everything else he said, he told her he didn't know anything of a Ms. and Mr. Nelson; he had been living here for three months already and knew nothing of the previous inhabitants. Ythoda almost shouted that that was impossible, that she had seen them just this morning, Ms. Nelson seeing Mr. Nelson out on his way to work and both of them waving at her when they noticed her looking out of her bedroom window. But she held , knowing that it would be useless to attest to their having been living there only that morning. From the way he actually looked up when she questioned him, offended surprise overshadowing his fear just that little moment, it was obvious that, as far as he was concerned, the man was not lying. Besides, at closer inspection the garden did look as if it had been under his clumsy care for months. The roses that had been blooming lusciously that morning were now drooping and dry; the hedge was pruned, but irregularly, not straight as a whistle as it had always been and the grass was much longer than Mr. Nelson would ever have allowed it to grow. No, the garden was definitely nothing like it had been that morning, Ms. Nelson's pride.

In view of the evidence, Ythoda hung her head and turned away; the cold, no, the fear that had begun nestling in her stomach what seemed an eternity ago, was now spreading all through her body, making her shiver with the chill of it, numbing her fingers and her toes, making her tongue hang limply in her dry mouth and bringing the first tears to her eyes. Finally, she could do nothing but admit to herself that she was afraid, that the thing she had always feared most seemed to have come true.

Had she stopped to consider everything that had transpired in the last hour or so- not seeing anybody she knew, Frank and her mother nowhere to be found and now this- perhaps at that point it should already have been obvious to her that, even though the place she was in was the spitting image of her town, she had never really made it home. It should have been clear to her that someone was playing an elaborate trick on her, one that would be in very bad taste if it were a joke. After all she wasn't a stupid child and, rationally at least, she knew full well that it was impossible to swap all the people she knew without her noticing anything.

But fear can do strange things to us. It can twist our perception so badly that we can't distinguish reality from imagination any more. It can make us believe that the things we know and see every day have suddenly been transformed into something very different, something that is not safe to be around. Fear isn't rational, and it prevents us from thinking on our feet or even with our eyes open.

So Ythoda didn't question that she really was where she thought she was. Now that she had finally admitted to her fear, it had gained such a grip on her that she was forced to believe that what her eyes saw, what her ears heard, was the truth and the truth alone.

That's why her mind hardly put up a fight when, when she turned to her "neighbour" again after having gathered all the courage she had left and asked about "the people next door," she heard that her parents had suddenly left a few weeks before. Her new neighbour didn't know why; they had never told him anything, he said. One morning, he had seen them put some suitcases into their car and drive away, just like that, and they hadn't returned so far. At first he had thought they were just on holiday, until the milkman came to his door asking whether they had left any money for him…

Ythoda was so aghast at the news that it didn't cross her mind to ask how it could be that there dust had accumulated anywhere, why her colour pencils were lying all across the coffee table or why the bread in the kitchen cupboard hadn't looked mouldy and, especially, how it was possible that her mother's purse was still there. In fact, none of those details came to her mind to aid her; she had pushed them away, forgotten all about them because they didn't fit into what her fear was forcing her to believe.

She began shaking and her eyes threatened to brim over, but she pushed the tears back. With a tight throat, her voice struggling to leave her body, she managed to ask: "But what about me?" The man looked directly at her this time, straight into her eyes, staring as if in shock, as if he couldn't believe his ears. He looked at her in complete silence for almost a full minute before, recovering his normal stance, he averted his eyes again.

"What about you?" he said "Who are you then?"

No, he had never seen their neighbours' daughter, never heard her or heard about her either, never heard her name shouted across the house, never heard doors slammed in anger... As far as he was concerned there had never been any sign of a child in that house and there definitely hadn't been a kid in the car with them that morning. If, despite all proof to the contrary, his neighbours had had a daughter, his guess was that they had just decided to leave her.

"Some parents do, you know."

19

The man didn't have any reason to lie to her.

It must be true then. It was all true. It had come to be, just as the darkest of her nightmares had always told her it would.

Devastated by what she had heard, her very existence denied to her face by someone who, as far as she was concerned, had never existed until a very short while ago, Ythoda turned her back to the man again and walked away from the fence, back to the road, through the garden gate next door. Dragging her unyielding feet, she tried to walk back to the house along the garden path, on what that very morning she had considered <u>her</u> garden path. She didn't make it to the door; halfway through a heavy step, her knees buckled beneath her and she found herself dropping down on the ground. She tried to get up, but her legs wouldn't support her; all strength seemed to have drained from them suddenly, as it had from the rest of her. Her hands hung limply at her sides, useless, her head drooped with its own weight and it was all she could do not to lie down in the middle of the path.

It was a strange feeling, that of her body suddenly not obeying her commands anymore, as if it had no strength to do so. She never had experienced something like that and couldn't really place it, especially as the cold feeling in the pit of her stomach, which had accompanied her since she left the House of Fear and which had so recently grown into a hurricane of fear raging through her being, was gone.

"That's odd," she thought, "I don't feel afraid any more."

It was true; she didn't feel scared any more. There is no need to fear the worst when the worst has already happened.

And the worst had happened to her, the thing she had feared most even if she had never completely realised it because it was so frightening that it became unthinkable. First, everybody she knew had disappeared. Then, her brother Frank, her twin, her constant ally and in every way an inseparable part of herself, had vanished. And now, it turned out her parents were gone without her, just like that, possibly even leaving her behind on purpose (though most of Ythoda couldn't believe that. No, someone must have been messing with their minds, somehow they really must have believed they had no daughter). Her parents, the people she had always been able to depend on no matter what and who had always loved her and supported her even if everyone else was against her had disappeared like a puff of smoke. Just as had everybody else

When the realization hit her, Ythoda doubled up in pain as her stomach contracted. It was a sharp pain, nauseating even, as if something had been torn out of her and she was bleeding inside. It was as if someone had thrust a knife into her belly and taken it out again, pulling her insides along with it, leaving her without any means to keep on living.

The pain grew and grew and became even worse as the fact that she was now completely alone became a litany that echoed in her mind over and over again. There was no one left to take care of her because, she was now utterly sure, there was no one in the whole world who knew who she was. She was a nobody, a homeless orphan without family or friends, and who in the world would want to take care of an unknown child? Who would love her how everybody she loved had left her?

She was all alone in the world; to her, there might as well not have been any other people in it anymore. To her it would have been just as bad had everybody suddenly died and had she been the only person left on the planet. In fact, that would have been better, because then she wouldn't have had to see other people loving and being loved while she looked at them from the sidelines, without any hope of love for herself.

Now that there was no longer a reason for its existence, the fear was gone and all that was left now was an all-pervading sense of loss, a feeling of despair that filled her completely: her body, her heart, her mind.

She couldn't think of anything to do. She didn't want to do anything either; deep in the recesses of her brain, she knew she should get up and try to find someone who could help her, that there were instances who would take care of her even if she was an unknown, unwanted, unloved child. But she just didn't want to: she didn't want to seek help and she didn't want to receive help either.

What would be the point anyway?

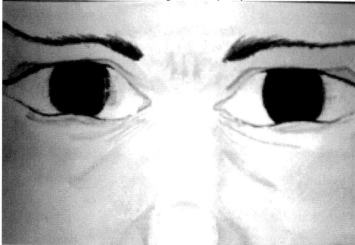

20

There was no point in doing anything, as there was no action in the world that would make any difference in her predicament, so Ythoda just sat where she had dropped down, in the middle of the garden path that was no longer hers, looking up at the house where she no longer lived. She sat, hugging her knees and rocking herself back and forth, back and forth, in the only motion that seemed as though it could keep her from dying of grief.

Still, the pain of her loss was growing steadily, becoming so great that she would almost have preferred having her insides torn out, just to escape what she was feeling right now. It was so strong, that it held her chest in an iron grip, preventing her from breathing properly, and it clogged her throat, not allowing her to cry out her agony. It covered her eyes with a muddy layer of sorrow, so she couldn't see clearly, and everything around her blurred; it pierced her brain with its incessant cry, so she couldn't think clearly, everything in her head muddled. Thoughts would begin to take form and explode again into nothingness as her sorrow screamed, "What are you thinking for? What makes you believe you have a future? Why would you even want to go on living?"

Ythoda just sat there, in the dirt, staring. She had stopped rocking herself an eternity ago; it didn't help, just as nothing else did. The pain had taken over, erasing her past, her present and her whole identity and nothing in the world was strong enough to heal it.

The world outside her pain was changing; it was getting darker and a wind had started to blow cold on her, but Ythoda didn't pay any attention to it, just as she didn't pay any notice to the stones that embedded themselves into the skin of her knees or the sand that had begun to blow into her eyes. At that moment, Ythoda was utterly unable to take heed of her body's sensations because she was too numb inside to feel any physical discomfort. And even if she had been able to feel it, she would still not have moved, not have done anything to feel less bad. She would just have sat there as she did now and everything would have gone on being blank.

Time didn't exist, the world didn't exist, life didn't exist.

She couldn't imagine herself doing anything anymore: not eating, not drinking, not finding a warm, dry place to sleep. Anything that would help her stay alive seemed like a far away possibility, something that might happen to other people but that wouldn't happen to her, couldn't happen to her because she didn't have either the strength or the will to make it happen. Somehow, Ythoda no longer wanted to live.

It wasn't really that she wanted to die either; she had just stopped wanting anything at all.

Sorrow has a way of filling you up until everything else is pushed out.

But, on the other hand, life has a way of making itself heard even through the worst sorrow and people's bodies often will fight to keep on living even if the person doesn't think she wants to.

So after a while, when it became apparent that her mind was in no condition to be in charge, Ythoda's body began, all of its own accord, to push the pain out it the only way a body knows how to when the brain won't cooperate. Without her willing it, her cheeks became wet with a moisture produced by her own body, that bitter liquid that is distilled of our grief and that rolls our of our eyes; her mouth began producing a high-pitched, formless sound. She didn't notice either thing.

They didn't soothe the pain.

Tears kept rolling down Ythoda's cheeks automatically, unchecked, dripping from her chin, falling on her lifeless hands and her knees forming wet patches on her trousers. Then, her body began what it had always felt was the most comforting motion of all and again she rocked back and forth, keening, completely oblivious to what she was doing.

But still the pain wasn't easing up, not really, not noticeably.

At that point, the sky had become so black as to seem almost night, even though sunset was still hours away; clouds had been accumulating in the sky above Ythoda's head, dark clouds of rain and thunder, covering the sun and hardly letting any of its light shine through.

It began to rain, large drops that fell on Ythoda's head, her back, her arms, the ground she sat on, the leaves on the trees, drumming on the rooftops and the cars in time with her keening and the splashing of her own teardrops on her body. The rain was falling in the same rhythm as her tears.

But Ythoda didn't notice the rain, just as she hadn't noticed the keening coming out of her own mouth, or the tears running down her own face; rain or shine, tears or not, it all was the same to her.

Her indifference, however, didn't affect the rain, which kept coming down on her and on everything around her, and soon she was soaked to the bone, wet through and through with rain from her eyes as well as from the sky.

But as the rain kept falling, the part of her that wanted to live despite her pain noticed something. It was not so much the wet, cold feeling of water running down her shirt and arms, or the "plic-ploc" of large drops falling on her head; the discomfort that she would normally have attached to those things was still too small, too unimportant to receive any attention.

What did stir her brain a little was how this was no normal rain: where normally, rain washed the air clear of the stench of the city and brought out the aroma of the grass and the flowers instead, this one had a strange smell to it, a bitter smell, the smell of sorrow. And, instead of tasting sweet like water that had been steeped in rose leaves, these drops had a salty taste, the same as the tears that came out of her eyes.

It wasn't raining ordinary drops, water the sun had evaporated from a river or the sea, or dew that was coming down before its time. It rained something else entirely.

It rained Ythoda's tears.

It was a downpour as she had never experienced before, the water a curtain that blurred the world even worse than her sorrow had, covering the irises of her eyes much more completely than her tears had.

Time had stopped, but the rain went on, relentless, as unrelenting as Ythoda's tears, and between the rain and the tears a puddle began to form around her, a bowlful of water that kept growing larger, slowly but steadily covering the ground around her: first just a little puddle around her feet, expanding to cover the path she was sitting on, then overflowing onto the whole garden, the street and the house. The puddle became a pool, became a lake, became a sea and soon it had covered everything and was beginning to rise.

It rose rapidly, like Noah's flood, and soon the water came up to her waist, then her chest, then her shoulders. Despite herself, despite her sorrow and her emptiness, a reflex made her stand up, but the water still kept on rising and rising.

At the rate it was going, it wouldn't take it long at all to cover her completely and soon after that, it would cover the whole world. Ythoda's sorrow was about to cover the whole world.

Who knew one could really drown in sorrow?

21

But a sorrow like Ythoda's is never endless as long as you can cry. Every tear takes with it a little of the pain until there's only as much left as your heart can cope with.

So little by little, tear by tear, Ythoda's heart did begin to feel lighter and as if by some cosmic law that connected the two, as the heaviness in her heart decreased, so did the speed at which the water rose.

At first, she fought against the easing of her grief, clinging to her sorrow as if it were some kind of paradoxical life-saver; having lost everything else, she didn't want to stop feeling the pain because that, she felt, would be to betray the memory of her vanished family and friends. As if letting go of the most excruciating part of her torment meant she was accepting her loss, and that was something she at that moment swore to herself she would never do. Because if she accepted what had happened to her, this crime that had been committed against her and her loved ones, she would be bowing her head to whomever had taken everybody she had ever cared about away from her for no reason, except just because they could and because they wanted to. If she accepted her loss, if she decided to learn to live with it even though it meant life-long unhappiness, it would mean victory to this mortal enemy she seemed to have.

The thing was, that Ythoda had never bowed her head to anybody who wanted to hurt her or anybody she cared about. Anybody who had tried to do so had always had had to pay with pain of their own. Anybody who had tried had at some point had to face the full force of Ythoda's anger.

Strangely, while one moment Ythoda thought all the feeling she had left in her was pain and despair and that she was completely helpless in the face of her fate, the next she realized that there was another way for her to cope, a way that would help her accept what had happened and at the same time still not let "him" (because now she was finally able to see at least this clearly, she knew full well who she meant, didn't shrink from the thought this time) win.

Not knowing how he had managed to exert his influence over her own world as well as his own and not understanding exactly what this power of his consisted of, let alone how it worked, Ythoda might not have the means to really get her own back on the Fearmaster; not only didn't she know what she could do to hurt him, she also didn't have a clue about how to reach him either. But one thing she was completely certain of, and that was that she would never let him win. She would not feed him with her fear any more, or with her sorrow for all that. She simply refused.

Her loss, her pain, her solitude, heavy as they were on her heart... they were <u>hers</u> and not his; he had had no right to cause her all the heartache she was suffering, no right to feed on it, let alone enjoy it, and Ythoda was going to make very sure he didn't. The very thought just...

And that was when Ythoda got angry, angrier than she had ever been in her life.

Rage rose in her from her toes upwards, rushing through her like a springtide of fury, pushing out the helplessness that had invaded her, even though the anger couldn't overshadow the pain. Her anger made her blood boil, electrified her limbs giving them a sudden injection of strength, made her hands itch and her scalp tingle, filled her throat with a howl that could not be kept back.

She got up in one bound as if impelled by a spring and let out her scream of rage, fists clenched, chest out, her face raised to the sky with her eyes closed, seeing her enemy on the inside of her eyelids as if projected on a movie screen. She did all of that out of sheer instinct, without thinking, without knowing why she was doing it, but feeling that it was the only way.

She didn't use any words, she didn't voice any thoughts; she didn't have to. All she had to say was: NO, NO, NO!

22

A nger is energy, an energy that can be directed at someone and blow them away without your even having to touch them.

The force of people's anger can hurt more than their fists would if they punched you. It's not for nothing that it is said that looks can kill; they might not literally do so, but someone else's anger can make you more than just uneasy. It can literally make you sick if the force with which it's directed at you is strong enough.

Ythoda's fear in the Fearmaster's house had already been tinged with anger, first because she was being kept out of what seemed a wild party, then at being forced to stay in a place where she no longer wanted to be. At that time, however, its energy hadn't been strong enough to be more than just an interesting new flavour for him, an interesting, exotic sauce to his food of choice. While her anger had just been a thin layer on top of her fear the Fearmaster had been able to feed on it as he was feeding on her fright and to read her soul in search of her deepest fear; at that moment, he was in complete control of her life and her will and she had indeed had no power against him at all.

The full force of her anger, however, was a completely different matter. It raged out of her like a tidal wave of destroying energy, moving at the speed of light; it collided against him like a wall, knocking him off balance, intending to seep into him through every pore in order to consume him from within and making him taste something he had never known he had. For the first time in his existence, the Fearmaster experienced a fear of his own, because the anger that was attacking him spoke of a hatred that wouldn't stop at anything, told him it would not cease until he was utterly destroyed. This rage was stronger than anything he had ever met, because he had never had to face anybody's fury in

Everwhere. And, unlike other feelings such as despair, sadness or even rebellion, he didn't know how to control rage and transform it into food, a nice little complement to his continuous meal.

His heart pounding with fright and dismay at the power that had been unleashed against him, the Fearmaster understood that he couldn't control the mind that was sending all that anger at him; it would be futile for him to try, and even a half-hearted attempt on his part would force him to release all other minds at the same time. So he had no choice but to give up.

The Fearmaster had finally encountered a power greater than his own, from a source he had never expected would possess it.

And so it came to be that the Fearmaster was forced to let go of Ythoda.

She had broken herself free without even knowing it.

Ythoda screamed until the howling in her brain, the racing of her blood, the bolts of lightning through her body had spent themselves. And as she did so, the rain, as well as her tears, stopped and the water receded until the sea became a lake, the lake a pool, the pool a puddle. Soon, the last drops around her feet evaporated while the last tears on her cheeks dried.

The world was still the same dreary place, still solitary, cold and dark; the sun was still covered by black clouds, but somehow they didn't look so menacing any more. Somehow, she knew even that the clouds and the cold wouldn't last forever; the sun might never again be as strong as it had once been, but it would come out again. Life would start again, from scratch if it had to.

She kept on screaming.

23

Ythoda sank back to her knees, exhausted, her eyes closed.

All her anger was spent for the moment, as were her tears; apparently, she had screamed out all of the former and cried all of the latter so completely that, if she had tried, she wouldn't have been able to imagine ever crying again.

Her soul was curiously empty, as if all feeling had been cleaned out of it, spent in tears and rage. The sense of utter futility and helplessness the despair had caused was gone and for the first time since disaster struck her, there seemed to be some room in her heart for hope and in her brain, for thought of something else than doom; had she wanted to, she would have been able to consider an action or maybe even a wish to do something. She didn't though; her recent ordeal had been so intense and taken so much of her strength that the lack of feeling she was experiencing now was almost enjoyable. It was a strangely peaceful sensation, calm and painful at the same time, not exactly pleasant but welcome nevertheless, if only for a while.

But only for a very short while.

After all, she was a child, not given to long reflection or prolonged periods of inactivity[34], and it only took a few minutes for her to begin to notice how cold she was, how tired and how sad. Now that

---

[34] "Prolonged" meaning more than, let's say, five minutes. That might not seem long at all, but let's face it, in a lifetime of little more than a decade, five minutes are a lot and children can cram a surprising amount of action or, rather, imagination in that time span.

Which is probably why it's so difficult to amuse a kid for more than that, especially if the amusement in question includes sitting still...

she had gone through the storm of her anguish and fury, life seemed an option again; she no longer wished for the world to stop turning and the whole of life to freeze forever but at the same time she realised that, as soon as she took her first step, she would begin to carry within her the memory of everyone she had lost for the rest of her life.

It wasn't an appealing thought, but she knew she would have to accept it, that not to accept it would mean giving up on living, and then the Fearmaster would have won again even if he had surrendered her.

But if she now got up and walked away, and found a way of making a life for herself, then he would have lost. Because then she would have faced what she had always thought, always known, was the worst that could happen to her and she would have survived; and that in its turn would mean that she would never need to fear again.

Ythoda might not be able to think this way yet, but there was one good thing about it all, which was that she would from now on be a truly fearless person; after all, there was nothing now that could faze her, no fate worse than what had already befallen her. Not even death…[35]

---

[35] Yes, I'm being serious here. We all tend to see death as the ultimate evil, which is only understandable, seeing as, whatever else it may be, it's the end of our experiences as <u>us</u>. But we all can think of situations where we would prefer for "us" to end rather than continue experiencing them; what Ythoda was going through is often one of them.

24

The shadows that had been covering the street, creeping forwards from the houses and reaching out to the children, as if trying to entrap them in their web of fright, had begun to retreat when Ythoda started screaming and now the street was bathed in a new light and the sun was shining full on her head. It wasn't only that, however: besides the new sunshine, which made sharp shadows on the street where the roofs protruded over the walls and which caused the windows to glitter like diamonds, there seemed to be a change in the atmosphere also. The silence was no longer leaden and dead, but was now coloured with the rustling of leaves, the buzzing of the occasional insect and even the chirping of a bird or two. There was also a new odour in the air, the smell of trees and flowers, the smell of people passing by, of children playing, of domestic animals: the smell of life.

And there was life, all around her: the windowsills had suddenly become populated with flowers, around which bees could be seen buzzing. Trees had sprung up fully grown, complete with birds nesting in them. The fountain in the square was no longer dusty and silent, but instead spouted clear water, gleefully singing in the midday sun. The church's weather vane was turning merrily in the breeze and the coloured windows reflected the light, shining with joy, inviting passers-by to come in and rest for a while. In the house across the square, the upstairs windows stood wide open, as they did in many of the other houses, which had suddenly become more real, like actual dwelling places, instead of masks trying fruitlessly to hide the Fear that had built the place

Ythoda hadn't taken in this sudden change; it was completely lost on her because her mind was busy perceiving quite different things. Now, with her eyes still closed, she couldn't see anything either, and therefore she was still unaware of where she was and of the change that had come over the place. But she did finally find herself able to feel the warmth that stole over her, telling her that things were different now, better; the sun shining on her head and on her upturned face told her that there was hope and that there still was something good to expect from life.

And then, out of the blue, a hand landed on her shoulder, warm and strong, its weight light on her. At the same time she heard a voice saying, "Ythoda, are you OK? Did you hurt yourself?"

The voice, Frank's voice, was full of concern, the hand, Frank's hand, comforting and full of love. His voice, his hand, she could feel in her whole being that they really cared. He really cared.

So then, why had he gone and left her? How dare he disappear like that and leave her to face her destiny alone, to go through hell all on her own? If he loved her so much, why wasn't he there for her when she needed him most?

Ythoda looked up, ready to lash out to him, her fury at the memory stronger than the relief at "finding" him again. But as she saw what had happened around her, she found herself unable to say a word. She couldn't even stand up; instead she shifted into a sitting position and simply stared, too baffled to do anything more than try to take it all in.

Because, contrary to what expected, she wasn't seeing her house from her garden path. The garden, the path itself, the house, the unknown neighbour weeding the plants at the other side of the fence, all of it had vanished as if by magic.

Instead, she saw the same square Frank and she had come out into when they rushed out of the Fearmaster's house, yet it was different. Because the shadows that had covered it before, seeming to come from the houses themselves, were gone and the sun was shining full on her head…

And Frank, who now crouched beside her, was looking at her intently, worried at her unresponsiveness, his hand still on her shoulder, shaking her lightly. "Ythoda, what's wrong? Are you hurt? Why aren't you saying anything?"

She looked at him, unbelieving, at loss for words for a moment. How could he say that? How could he ask that after…after she just had…almost…and then…?

And then the tears were back. "Where were you?" she sobbed, "I looked for you and you weren't anywhere!"

"What do you mean?" He sounded genuinely puzzled. "You just came rushing out of the house a moment ago, and then you tripped and fell"

Time doesn't pass in Everwhere.

That is how it was possible that while Ythoda was whisked away into a world made of her fears and had been forced to find a way to survive them and, in that way, free herself from both her fears and the Fearmaster, Frank had been right there. He had been there all the time, out of sight, out of earshot, out of reach and still only a heartbeat away.

It was mind-boggling.

She smiled at him while he helped her up. "I'm fine," she tried to lie. And then she almost winced when she saw him scrutinizing her with that quizzical look he always got when she was trying to pull one on him, except this time his expression was tinged with deep concern. Not that she was surprised; after all, she had never been able to lie to Frank. No matter how hard she tried, he always caught on almost before she had even started. Except this time, she would have given anything for him not to see through her, not out of shame over what she had been through or fear of his reaction, but because she had hoped that by ignoring what had happened, she would be able to put it behind her right away. Unfortunately[36] there was no way that was going to work with this

---

[36] Or maybe not so much. Ythoda had yet to realize that the pain of experiences like the one she had just had, of the kind that leave a scar in your soul even while transforming you, has a tendency to come back and haunt you until you have managed to deal with it completely.

twin of hers; what had she been thinking when she created a brother who knew her better than she knew herself?

Who, because he knew her so well, knew what had happened without her needing to say anything.

"He got to you, didn't he?" His asking was just a formality; he could see by the look on her pale face that it was so: the wide red-rimmed eyes, glazed over with shock, the tense mouth, the chin that pointed forward, as if challenging the world to dare say she had cried...Ythoda didn't need to speak at all; she only had to nod. "So what happened? Did everyone you know abandon you?"

"Something like that." Which was already an incredibly open admission for Ythoda, as normally there would have been no force in the world that could make her admit to fearing anything, not to anybody, not even to herself. But this was not a normal time and, after all, it doesn't do to be cocky when you've just faced your worst fear and barely come out of it alive. Ythoda was completely conscious of this, realizing full well that she was in dire need of her brother's support and knowing that she must admit to her fear in order to receive that support.

On his part, Frank forbore to push her any further, not asking for more explanation than that. Ythoda was grateful for this consideration, relieved that she didn't have to explain; it was bad enough to feel so weak and needy, bad enough to carry the memory of the emotional roller coaster she had been on not only in her brain, but also through her whole body. The last thing she wanted now was to have to think about it, to put it all in words forcing, herself to relive the whole thing. She just didn't have the strength.

She knew she would have to talk to Frank at some point, that he wouldn't continue to be content to be there for her without knowing what had actually happened. But not now. Right now, all she wanted was to enjoy not being alone.

25

She got more of her wish than she had expected.

Because something else was different in the village: where before there had only been empty houses in a deserted street, now the place was teeming with life. Sounds came out of windows and open doors, curtains fluttered in the breeze, as did the leaves of the trees that seemed to have sprung up so suddenly. Birds sang and voices sang with them from inside the now welcoming houses.

And there were people too, everywhere, all around the twins on the street, going in and out of the houses, greeting each other, stopping to talk to each other and scolding their children for running around and bumping into people. The shops, which before had been empty shells, now sold their wares, if the people entering them and leaving again with their arms full were any indication; and all around, people went about their business, whether it was work or leisure, with the kind of cheerfulness which springs from knowing who you are and where you belong.

In all, what Ythoda and Frank were witnessing was no more a normal scene in a normal street (for some kind of historical theme park), with normal (meaning "human-looking") people.

The strangest, but also the most marvellous, thing was that they all behaved as if they had always been there, while the children knew very well that the whole town had been completely empty until all these people, all this life, appeared out of thin air just a moment ago.

It was a great, heart-warming moment for the children. The town had suddenly become a welcoming place, a place where they would definitely not mind lingering for a little while because despite all the differences it felt almost like home.

Unless…

Was this really so? Were they really seeing all this or was it all their imagination again? Was something like this really possible? Could it be?

Or was this just another trick of the Fearmaster, to lull them into unwatchfulness, to make them think they were safe just so he could twist it all in his own evil way, so that he could play with them again? For a moment, Ythoda felt a pang of cold, but it didn't last long.

For she just had to look into the eyes of the people to see that all of this was not, could not be, a figment of <u>his</u> mind. Because, where in the reality Ythoda had just left all of his creations had looked at her and at each other just as the "guests" in the House of Fear had, full of fear and shame, these people looked each other in the eye without hesitation, with the confidence of people who knew each other and were sure they could trust their fellows. There was no fear in those eyes, no mistrust, no shame.

These were no slaves of a harmful master, living in fright and despair, but real people, free people, just like Frank and Ythoda herself.

Hopefully they would turn out to be friendly people as well, she thought.

She wished.

And then, there was a man coming towards them, smiling broadly, his arms open in a welcoming gesture. He reached the spot where the children were standing and embraced them warmly, fondly, as if he were some cheerful, loving uncle and they his long-lost niece and nephew. Taking a step back, though still holding their shoulders, he then surveyed them intently, scrutinizing their faces with a friendly yet serious gaze, as if trying to read what had happened to them.

His stare, though intense, didn't feel uncomfortable to Ythoda and Frank; there was too much warmth in it, too much genuine concern for it for them to consider it intrusive or even unsettling.

At last, the man's eyes left their faces with a satisfied sigh and his tense features relaxed into an expression of beatific happiness. When he spoke, his voice beamed along with his smile.

"Ah, it is so good to see both of you alive and well," he told the bewildered twins, who had no idea what this stranger could possibly mean by that. "It's not often people escape 'the other place' and when they do they usually never are…" Here, the man interrupted himself abruptly, as if he had just been about to divulge something that must never come out.

"But never mind that now… You must be exhausted, you poor lambs. Well, no matter, we will take care of you…or I will, for now anyway. Let's go to my house, shall we? You can have a rest before the gathering at sunset today and, oh dear," he added, noticing the state of Ythoda's hair and clothing. "You sure can use a bath, can't you?…And clean clothes, though of course I don't really have any clothes your size…I'm going to have to try out the Washer…it wasn't working properly last week but with the new adjustments…" Still chattering in his somewhat rambling manner, their new friend steered the children towards a side street that had also suddenly erupted when they left the inn and where his cottage apparently stood.

It was a house pretty much like all the others, small and quaint, painted a bright blue with white woodwork. While on the main street the houses' front doors opened directly into it, on this little side street they all had small front gardens; and the twins couldn't repress a smile at the clutter their host had managed to accumulate in his, very much in contrast to the other, perfectly kept yards.

Now, of course Ythoda had been taught by her parents never to go home with a stranger, and she never would have done such a thing, were it not that this man didn't seem like a stranger at all, even if she had never seen him before. It wasn't only the way he had greeted them, as if he had known them all their lives, or the decisive way in which he took charge of them, much like a mother hen[37] cluck-clucking around her chicks; it was everything else as well. All about him felt familiar, and comfortable and friendly: not only his beaming round face, his warm low voice or the twinkle in his kind eyes, but there was also something indefinable there. Something about him, about the way he moved, the way he spoke, made you feel you could trust him with your life. And his round, blue eyes too shone with a special light, looking at the world with a friendly sort of

---

[37] Which, granted, was a bit of a strange thing in a man. But let's face it; they had been through too many strange things already to wonder at a little thing like that… Besides which, why should we hold on to useless role-patterns anyway? It was nice, and at this time, that was all that mattered to the twins.

wonder that made you feel this man had a very special kind of heart; it was almost as if you could look into his eyes and see all of his soul- and it was wholly good, full of love for everything and everyone around him.

His name was George Whatnot and, as it turned out, he knew all about the Fearmaster.

In fact, as he told them later over a cup of tea and some cake, everybody in the village knew about the boy and about what they had come to call "the other place;" they had never seen "him" and everybody in town was very careful not to set foot in the Inn, well aware of which trap lay for them there. They knew all about the despair that ruled that place and about the Fearmaster's unfortunate slaves, condemned to feed him with their fear until their deaths.

No one liked to talk about it; it was too awful a thing to be discussed, too horrifying to do anything but try to ignore it. But they all knew what it meant when someone suddenly appeared out of nowhere in the middle of the street, just in front of The House. The Inn stood empty here, he explained, but it was common knowledge that there was another side to the town; a parallel village almost, but not quite, an exact replica of their own, where people who happened to wander into it almost always got trapped in The House and mostly never came out. Some, not many, did escape, however, but unfortunately (George's face grew quite sad when he said this) even fewer made it to his side alive. Then, their bodies appeared on the Inn's doorstep bearing no marks of whatever caused their death but the expression on their faces, which suggested they had died of fright. It was a sad, sad thing, especially because since Fear Town had been created, in his great-grandfather's time, no one had ever escaped that most terrible of fates...

But, and now his face brightened, the two of them had and that was cause for celebration. Would they care for more cake?

26

Cake might not seem like much of a way to celebrate a momentous occasion like their victory over the Fearmaster clearly was, but as it turned out, it was not by far all Ythoda and Frank got by way of a party.

Because the tradition of the village was that, if someone ever managed to break free from Fear Inn, the whole town would get together to celebrate the victory and the lucky escapees would become honorary citizens of the town from there onwards.

The villagers regarded the Fearmaster as their worst enemy because he was using a corrupted, yet incredibly accurate, copy of their beloved town as his own personal spider web, to catch hapless travellers who thought they had reached the safety of the Village but instead, through some unknown enchantment, lost their freedom and their life forever. It wasn't every traveller who got caught that way; mainly, the victims consisted of people who were lost and who didn't know the Village existed. But sometimes, someone the villagers knew disappeared into Fear Town and there had been some cases of inhabitants of the Village being enslaved as well.

That in itself was reason enough for the people to hate the Fearmaster, but there was another reason as well, which was that word of the trap was beginning to spread into the countries of Everwhere and the Village was beginning to be avoided by strangers. This cut the people off from the rest of the Land in a way that was making trade more and more difficult, and causing young people to want to leave so they could escape the menace that always hung over their town as well as meet new people which would otherwise have come to them.

Other than putting up road signs and warnings, there was nothing the people could do to stop the Fearmaster's evil work so instead they became the most hospitable town in Everwhere, welcoming every traveller who made it to the Village instead of Fear Town as if they were long lost friends.

And it had long ago been decided that, if anybody ever managed to break the power that bound them there and escape with their lives, there would be a festival like the town had never known before to celebrate the first known victory over their greatest enemy.

So that night[38] a bonfire was lit in the main square in front of the church. The town's band played every tune they knew and the whole Village danced around the fire; later on, when the flames subsided a little, some of the most daring boys and girls amongst the town's youth would jump over the fire and so did the twins, cheered on by one and all.

This was all after sunset, of course. Just before, there had been a whole function with speeches, songs and all kinds of entertainment which had gone on until just before it all got boring, followed by a huge feast to which everybody but Frank and Ythoda contributed something (her offer to do so had been met with shocked rejection and besides, her pocket-money really was of no use here) and took away a very full belly indeed.

The celebration was concluded with a marvellous display of fireworks George had prepared them and they were nothing like the children had ever seen; they lasted for the longest imaginable time, if such a thing had existed in Everwhere, and shone with all the colours of the rainbow and a few more in between, exploding in the air in the shape of flowers and stars, trees and animals, castles, dancing couples and even a dragon or two.

The sun had already begun to rise when the last sparks died away.

And then, finally, sleep.

---

[38] Yes, we did say time doesn't pass in Everwhere. But as people can't conceive the world without day and night, both also existed there. Not at a set pace, however; days and nights could be longer or shorter according to the needs of the people, and they could come at different times in different places. Very confusing.

In this case, night was called for as soon as the preparations for the party were done, and that didn't take any time at all.

Literally.

27

It was full daylight again when Ythoda woke up in George's house. Breakfast was on the table when she got down to the kitchen, but there was no one there. The room seemed to suddenly go dark and Ythoda went pale; the night before, with all the partying and the fun, she had managed to put her experience at the Fearmaster's mercy out of her mind, or so she thought. But now, stepping into an empty kitchen, not knowing where her brother had gone, or George for that matter, it all came rushing back to her: the disappearance of her parents and of all the people she knew, the fear, the sadness and the terrible feeling of abandonment and helplessness. For one short moment, she felt the flood of tears that had almost cost her her life flow around her once more and thought "he" must have caught up with her at last. A scream welled up in her throat and got caught there, fear threatening to invade her again; but then, she remembered the rest of it as well. In a flash, she re-lived her defiance of her tormentor and the feeling of freedom that had come over her when she realized that, no matter how desperate her situation looked, she was alive and stronger than any fear or pain...

Nevertheless, relief washed over her when she heard muffled voices coming from behind a door at the other side of the hallway; listening intently, she could make out George's low voice and booming laughter and Frank's higher tones. She couldn't understand what they were talking about, but it definitely sounded like they were having a lot of fun. Too much fun for such an early hour.

Normally, Ythoda, who was not a morning person, would for once have left the fun to Frank and sat down to a leisurely breakfast by herself before joining him; and the spread George had left for her on the table would have assured her of a very leisurely meal indeed. Now, however, she couldn't stand the thought of being alone for even a little while, not yet, not until she was completely sure the people she loved wouldn't leave her again; so she grabbed some cakes that had been left over from the party (and which were surprisingly fresh after a whole night out- just one more perk of timelessness) and went to look for her brother.

She found him together with George in a room across the hall at the front of the house. They were sitting amidst what she would herself have called a pile of junk: strange objects were lying everywhere, filling up every one of the shelves that lined the walls, and piling up on the floor, leaving no space uncovered. Some of the things were clearly machines, a few of which pretty familiar-looking, such as a large square apparatus with a round door in the middle that bore a label that read "Washer"; Ythoda remembered George mentioning it not being all too reliable, but, judging by the pristine status of her clothes, which she had found neatly folded by her bed when she woke up, this time it had worked fine.

Most of the items strewn around, however, bore no resemblance to anything that could be of any use, with the possible exception of a box of bolts and clogs that was sitting next to the door.

The clutter made the room all but impracticable and the dust covering everything made her eyes sting and her nose itch, but that didn't seem to bother either George or Frank as they inspected some strange object placed on a table.

From the door, she couldn't make out what it was or, to be more precise, what it resembled, so she moved to get closer, dust flying up at every step and every inevitable brush of some object or other lying in her path. The other two looked up at hearing her sneeze, Frank's face beaming with excitement. "Do you know what this is?" Ythoda shook her head. "It's a machine that will take you anywhere in Everwhere. George made it and it actually works! We tried it before you came down and it was great! George went to the baker's in the next town to get some bread and was back before I could even blink and then I went over to the…"He stopped abruptly at the suddenly sad expression on her face. "You don't mind, do you?" he added more soberly, the recollections from the previous day suddenly springing up in his mind.

She did mind, a little, not because she had missed out on anything but because it meant he had left her alone- and, even if she had never noticed, that did make her feel a sort of sadness; nothing much, just a faint echo of what she had felt before. But she didn't want to go into it so she just shook her head and approached the table to take a closer look at the machine. It was hard to describe, something like a crossing between a remote control and a blow dryer but then much bigger and with some kind of steering wheel added to it, made of different kinds of metal and plastic of different colours. It was clearly made of bits and pieces of everything and definitely didn't look as it could do anything but be in everybody's way to break their shins on.

But judging by Frank's red-faced excitement, the device actually worked, and he clearly couldn't wait to show her. "So, where do you want to go next?" he asked, "George says he will take us wherever we want to go. Would you like to visit The Palace?"

At any other time, Ythoda would have jumped at the chance to visit a palace, never mind what it was- of course, she would have asked what The Palace was (never mind how Frank managed to pronounce the capitals of the name) before going there, just for her own information, but she wouldn't have thought twice about the wisdom (or stupidity) of going there[39].

At that moment, with everything that had happened still fresh in her mind, it was all she could do not to cry at the thought of going to another new place, visiting somewhere else she didn't know; perhaps to meet people she hadn't before and maybe even to face the dangers that hadn't crossed her mind before and that Frank couldn't imagine[40].

From the moment she had broken free of the Fearmaster, she had been pretending that everything was OK now, like a child will when something is over and she partly knows, partly wants to convince herself it's not going to come back. During the party, she had made a great show of enjoying herself, dancing, eating, laughing, jumping over the fire, pretending all that had happened had been of no consequence at all to her, that there had been nothing to it. She had been trying to convince herself and everybody else along the way that, now she knew that all she had been through had been a fiction created by the Fearmaster to bring her to her knees, she didn't need to go home and check that everybody

---

[39] But as she didn't ask, you'll need to know, for future reference, that the Palace is the place where the Powers of Everwhere reside. Everybody knows it, and everybody manages to pronounce the name with capitals.

It's the easiest address ever.

[40] For obvious reasons.

was still there and that her parents hadn't gone anywhere. She had almost succeeded in believing that she didn't really need her mum that much, that knowing Mum was there and that she could go home to her any time she wanted was enough to make her feel safe.

Almost, but not quite.

In fact, she did want to see her mother very badly. She had wanted to see her from the moment she knew everything was all right and that she hadn't really been left all alone in the world- but she hadn't wanted to give in to the feeling, not with all the exciting things that were happening there and then. Not with Frank looking at her and worrying about her, making her feel like he was the one taking care of her, like she was helpless and weak when it had always been she who was the strong one.

Now, she gave in.

"I just want to go home", she whispered. And again, "I want to go home".

It wasn't just a wish, it was an urge, an ache, a need that wouldn't admit any delay; and where before she had been quite content to do things in what she, and everybody else, considered the normal way, that is to say, by walking on her own feet and using her own hands and mind, now the thought of having to feel Everwhere's non-existing time rushing by while she got to her destination was more than she could bear.

And it was this burning longing that helped her remember the power she had in Everwhere, about making the fairies appear and disappear and about being able to make anything happen by just using the right words, so she cried them out

"I wish I was home right now!" And she waited, expectantly, defiantly, as if challenging the Land to give her what she wanted and to do it NOW.

Nothing happened.

Why was nothing happening? She looked at Frank and then at George, her face demanding an explanation. They had one for her, one she didn't like at all.

Wishes, they said, can make things appear for her in Everwhere, but they can't take you out of it. That would mean Ythoda's wishes had an influence on her world as well and it's quite clear to see why that wouldn't do at all.

Ythoda was thrown for a moment, then started thinking intensely, frowning, racking her brain for a new quick fix to her problem.

"Ok, then I wish we were at the door we came in through."

Again, nothing. Why wasn't it happening? Why weren't her wishes coming true just when she needed it the most? Why couldn't she go home instantly like she wanted? This wasn't funny any more.

Ythoda's eyes misted over, her lips started to tremble. She didn't want any more adventures, any more travelling; she didn't want to deal with any delays, of any kind. It all was more than she could bear.

"I can't do this," she wailed. "I can't walk all the way to the door, I can't wait...I...I just can't". A tear rolled down her cheek and her shoulders started to shake.

Frank hastened to put his arm around her shoulders, comforting and steadying her. "No, please, don't cry. You don't need to cry. You won't need to wait either; really, we can get to the door right away. That's what the machine is for, remember? It can take us there without us having to walk. That is what we tried it out for, to make sure it would work, so we could get to wherever you wanted to go next".

She relaxed a little, relieved but still pouting. "Oh. OK. But why won't my wishes work?"

It has already been said that Everwhere has laws, meant to keep things and events from running into each other because, like in our reality, two things can't coexist in the same place[41]; if that ever happened, the Land would explode- which would be a very, very bad thing to happen, as every Everwherian would agree.

One of the laws is the law of distance. It means that things that already exist can't be moved to a completely different place just by wishing[42] from inside the Land; that was because the wisher had no way of knowing if something or someone else was already located at the same exact spot. On the other hand, when something new is wished or created

---

[41] Well, Ok, so Fear Town did. Apparently, the Fearmaster or whoever came up with him found a loophole to that particular law; good for them.

[42] Which is why so many beings in Everwhere have wings. They need them.

from the outside, Everwhere just expands ever so little to make space for the new arrival, thus ensuring there is no collision…and no explosion.

Therefore, Ythoda and Frank would either have to walk all the way to their door or, seeing as there were no horses or other creatures what would carry them available, create a car. Which would have been a great idea had either of them been able to drive.

And that's where George's invention came in. He couldn't really explain how it was possible, but he had invented the Instant Mover, a machine that could "fold" Everwhere so distance would disappear for all practical purposes. It didn't involve any appearing or disappearing, but was more like taking a very giant step in a very small one.

No one noticed it when that happened, for some reason not even the Wardens, and it seemed to be completely safe.

So it looked like Ythoda would get her wish after all, it would just not happen in the usual, "poof-there-we-are" way.

She didn't mind.

28

Not surprisingly, the door was just where they had left it.

Well, actually, they should have been surprised.

At any rate, Frank an George definitely would have, had they known that the Wardens of the Land, those entities that had been created to make sure the laws were respected and that the borders weren't compromised, were now fully aware of Ythoda's presence in Everwhere and because of it were panicking about what to do with her[43].

The thing was, she should never have been there in the first place, for reasons that have already been disclosed; but now she was there and the Wardens had no way of getting rid of her, seeing as Ythoda was completely out of their power. Nevertheless, they had to find a way of preventing her going back into her world and blabbing about the Land everywhere, preferably without hurting her in the process. It was bad enough having one human kid about, happily wishing something to appear here and something gone there and threatening to upset the order

---

[43] Although "panic" might be a rather strong word to describe their reaction; their response to the news hadn't caused any screaming, flailing of arms, tearing of hair or any such response. It had been more like raising an eyebrow and coolly acknowledging to each other that they were utterly at loss about what to do next.

No big deal except that, for beings "blessed" with an utter lack of imagination, it was pretty much imperative that they know pretty much every possible move for every possible contingency.

So I guess "panic" might be a good word after all.

of things[44], having a whole invasion of them really wouldn't do. The Wardens couldn't see how she could be prevented from going and bringing over all her little friends so they could all run around wreaking havoc together. And it would be even worse if any adults got wind of Everwhere and decided to come and check it out; it didn't take an imagination to know that it would be a disaster once some of them, or even one, began to "put things in order", as they would no doubt be calling it.

So, seeing as they hadn't been able to keep the girl out, they must now keep her in at all cost. Anything rather than allowing a melting of the two worlds: Everwhere and the reality that had spawned it.

Of course, the Wardens didn't really need to worry: they might not be able to picture more than one possibility of what would happen if she talked, but Ythoda was more than smart enough to realise that she would never be able to tell anybody. Not if her goal wasn't to tell a story for someone's amusement but to make Everwhere pass as a real place in people's minds. It was not so much that nobody would believe her, though it was clear to her they wouldn't; the real problem, and the effect she wanted to avoid, was that they would probably think her insane, a thought that didn't appeal to her at all. After all, she was already considered "weird" (by some of the kids) or just "strange" (by some of the adults, more diplomatic in their words if not in their thinking) because of what people saw as an excess of imagination; if she began talking about some place made of imagination as if it were real, there would be no stopping her parents from getting her a kind of "help" she really, really didn't want to receive.

No chemical lobotomy for Ythoda, that much she was determined about.

Besides which, she wasn't really sure if it would do for people (Ythoda counted herself out of the human race just for this one) to go traipsing about a place like Everwhere and getting themselves in trouble

---

[44] Ythoda hadn't, not really. But she had left one or two traces they couldn't do anything about and to the Wardens, everything they couldn't control was such an upset.

In that sense, they had a lot in common with some of the older members of the human race.

over wrong wishes and all that. And not only the kids, she knew, it was the adults who would be especially bad[45].

In all, she had more reasons to keep her adventure quiet than to tell anybody about them. And after all, why would she want to anyway? Right now, at least, all she wanted was to go home and never come back to Everwhere, and even forget about the Land if she possibly could.

No, as far as Ythoda was concerned, no one in her world would ever hear of Everwhere, not from her anyway. It just wasn't in her best interest, not right now nor, of this she was sure, would it ever be.

Still, the Wardens didn't know any of this; how could they, if none of them had ever even set eyes on Ythoda, let alone spoken to her? On the other hand, even if they had been aware of her state of mind, they wouldn't have believed her silence would last, if she managed to keep one to begin with. They had just enough knowledge about human psychology to know that people like to talk about their experiences, especially if, like Ythoda's (which they did know about, by the way) they are of the life-changing type; and it's a well known fact that often the need to tell about something can overcome all prudence.

The Wardens were sure that was true for pretty much every human being alive and to keep it from happening to Ythoda, they were very kindly trying to devise a way to keep her in Everwhere.

---

[45] And that was pretty much the only thing Ythoda and the Wardens would ever agree about.

29

Surprisingly, the door was still there when they arrived in George's Instant Mover.

Unsurprisingly for us (though it came as quite a shock for them), there was a Warden posted right in front of it.

"*******" Said Frank. George agreed wholeheartedly.

The Warden came forward, walking stiffly, its back straight as a rack, its knees unbending as if it had none, which was actually the case, its hand raised in a stop sign.

Impossible as it may seem, Wardens have no gender at all; they look pretty much like those small dolls with no joints that can be cast in any role in a child's game: their arms and legs cannot bend, and neither can their backs. They all have a kind of longish brown helmet which must pass for hair, a small nose, a big mouth, apple cheeks and round eyes devoid of any expression. Their torso is cylindrical and smooth and they wear a kind of uniform, consisting of grey pants and a kind of grey tunic. They all look exactly alike, sound exactly alike and act exactly alike in like situations; they not only do not have a gender, they have no identity at all.

The Warden guarding the door stopped a few steps from where Ythoda was standing together with her brother and George; its hand was still raised, palm forward. It spoke in a flat, high-pitched voice.

"Thou shall not pass" it said earnestly, completely unaware of how ridiculous it sounded, and just stood there, feet slightly apart, hand still raised, no expression at all on its face.

Something about it put Ythoda in mind of a traffic regulator: annoying (according to her father) but useful when you didn't want traffic to become chaos (according to her mother). It was surprising to see something like that here, but nothing in its looks or demeanour gave her any reason to be afraid, not that she could see; which is why she couldn't really understand why Frank and George looked ashen all of a sudden.

Until she tried to move forward towards the door and found herself bumping into an invisible wall; it didn't exactly hurt, but she did feel an unpleasant tingling where her body had touched the...whatever it was.

She looked at the Warden, who was looking at her unmovingly; in reaction to her move, it flicked its hand and for a moment Ythoda thought she saw the air shimmer, forming the invisible wall she had bumped into and thickening it even further. Apparently, the Everwhere traffic regulator was in earnest.

Still, she tried to go forward once more, with the same results.

"Thou shall not pass", said the Warden again.

"Why?" she demanded.

No one ever questioned a Warden; they strict upholdance of the laws was very well known, as was the fact that they had the power to keep any being from breaking one. All Everwhere knew that they had the capacity to do awful things to one, so terrible that everybody preferred not to find out exactly what those things were. In actual fact, these horrid things existed mostly in the word-of-mouth of the people[46] than in reality and the Wardens were quite happy to keep it that way. It kept people from breaking the rules and them to have to run to the Powers so they could devise a fitting punishment for the Wardens to deal out; they would, if necessary, of course, but it was sooo much hassle...

At any rate, Ythoda did question the Warden, which, not being used to having to answer to anything, didn't really know what to say; it would have, except no one had told it why it was guarding the door, just that it had to. So it tried an approach it had heard was quite common amongst human parents and which it hoped would work here too.

---

[46] We can't say in their imagination, because, as we all know, imaginary beings have no imagination

"Because I said so" It tried to put as much conviction in its voice as it could.

Ythoda was not convinced. "That's a stupid reason if I ever heard one! Now, would you be so kind as to let me through? I want to go home!" She paused for a moment, to see if what she said had any effect and, seeing it didn't, repeated it again, with a slight, yet important variation: "I wish to go home"

That put the Warden in a pickle. True, it had orders not to let Ythoda through on any account; but on the other hand, she had just uttered a wish and it was a deeply ingrained principle in every Warden that human wishes had to be respected. Everwhere was built on wishes and if a wish wasn't allowed to come true- any wish that was in keeping with the laws, that is- the ensuing chain reaction could endanger the whole structure of the Land. It was a loose-loose situation.

The Warden hesitated, unprepared to deal with such an uncommon situation. "One moment", it mumbled. And disappeared.

Taking her chance, Ythoda ran forward.

Unfortunately, the invisible wall was still in place.

"Ouch", said Frank.

30

Ythoda saw stars before she saw the Warden; it had been gone no time at all. She shook her head, as the blow seemed to have blurred her vision; the Warden seemed to waver, it's contours shaky, as if out of focus, and for a moment she thought she saw double, another blurry figure having materialized next to it.

When she managed to focus her eyes a little better, she saw it hadn't doubled itself after all, but returned accompanied by something, no, someone else. At the sight of it, George gasped.

"It's one of the Powers", whispered Frank, awestruck. "But what is she doing here? This is incredible! They never leave the Palace unless it's an emergency and they hardly ever speak to people in person, unless... Ythoda, you must be very important."

Frank was clearly amazed and even without knowing anything about the Powers, Ythoda too was duly impressed. The Powers are the highest authority in Everwhere, the only ones with the power to bypass the laws and the only beings in the Land with the capacity to create things by just whishing them. Contrary to the Wardens, Powers do have genders, and the one standing before Ythoda was the most dazzling woman she had ever seen. Quite literally: everything about her, from her indigo-blue gown to her waist long blue hair, sparkled as if covered in diamonds; except that she wore no such thing. The sparks of blue fire dancing around her were caused by her own power, so great that it couldn't always be contained, becoming visible in a shower of light. She stood tall, very tall, and proud, her indigo coloured eyes irradiating such force one could hardly imagine looking into them. The power that surrounded her, the strength of her gaze, made it hard to see her features sharply, but even so, it was clear to see that she was beautiful. Unearthly beautiful and immensely powerful.

The lady took a step forward and bowed her head slightly in a proud salute. Her movements were graceful, her slim figure and long, slender arms dancing like a tree in a breeze. Her copper coloured skin was smooth like a girl's and her features too were that of a young woman.

On the surface, she looked very young, almost so young she could have been Ythoda's sister, and for a moment, Ythoda wished she was. In fact, the Indigo lady was the youngest of the seven Powers, the last one to have come into existence, but despite that, there was a timeless quality about her too, as if she were young and ancient at the same time, both her beauty and her power seeming to stem from before the beginning of time[47].

Ythoda scrambled quickly to her feet, feeling very insecure. Although she didn't really understand what the whole fuss was all about, she was beginning to realise that this blocking her way to the door wasn't just another "cute" trick of the Land to tease her a little before she went home. When the one preventing her from reaching the door was the Warden, with it's traffic guard look, she hadn't really taken it seriously: the being was too much like a playmobil doll for Ythoda to see it as anything but a pushover and she had expected to be done with it with no effort at all.

However, the Power was a completely different matter. For one, her presence made it clear to Ythoda that the whole situation was a serious affair, a matter of state, not something she could dismiss lightly or at all. Also, here was someone with the authority and the power to supersede human wishes, someone who could and would take matters in hand and Ythoda wasn't at all confident that things would end up going her way.

The woman's face was hard to read or, rather, too changeable to give an idea of what she might be thinking. One moment, her expression was stern and unmoveable; the next, her face would soften and her eyes fill with compassion. She stood straight and tall, radiating a power that would have been fearsome had it not been wrapped in kindness. Hers was not the power to do harm; severe as she could look, there was no hint of evil in her sternness. Ythoda had nothing to fear from her.

---

[47] And, if time had existed in Everwhere, that would have been exactly the case.

And yet, she had everything to fear from her…

"So you wish to go home?" The Power's voice was soft, kind, warm. It caressed you, wrapped you up like a blanket and made you feel cared for, completely safe. It was the kind of voice that told you that it completely understood how you were feeling and felt for you and would help you if it could. But it also told you you'd better not cross her when she had made up her mind. Because if you probed beyond the warm, fuzzy blanket feeling its tones created, you would find that it would go only where it wanted to, do only what it wanted to and there would be nothing you could do to stop it. In all its softness, that voice had steel underneath.

And in that steel undertone, Ythoda heard very clearly that Everwhere wasn't planning to let her go. It wasn't angry with her with her for coming and neither did it mean her any harm. In fact, it really wanted to help her and make her happy. But always IN Everwhere, not outside it.

Ythoda felt herself go weak with dismay; she didn't know exactly where all this was going, but it definitely wasn't going to be home.

The Power went on. "Well, don't worry, we're working on it".

This last remark came as a complete surprise to Ythoda, and Frank's eyes went wide as well. They were working on it? They were working on letting her go home, on giving her what she wanted? Why all this "Thou shalt not pass, then? Why the Warden and its invisible wall? Why make her believe they were going to keep her and then change their minds, just like that?

Ythoda was flabbergasted. After all the display of power she had witnessed, with the Power's voice telling her without so many words that she couldn't go, now she was being told…that? She wanted to believe it meant what she wanted it to mean, but it all was too discrepant, too inconsistent. Still, she had to take her chance now, before the Land changed its mind again.

"Euh…so I can just…?" Ythoda took a few timid steps towards the door- the Warden didn't even let her reach the invisible wall this time.

"Thou shalt not pass", it said for the third time. It was beginning to look bored with it.

The Power laughed, a light, silvery laugh like a sunbeam on water that made Ythoda want to slap her. This was not the time to be all cute and fairylike, for Heaven's sake! Not when her whole future was at stake!

The laugh stopped- Power might look and sometimes act like fairies, but they are far from stupid or insensitive. Silvery laughs aren't always the best way to put someone at ease; they clearly didn't work with this girl- the Power liked her all the better for it.

So instead, she went on to explain that Ythoda could never go to the "real" world again now she not only knew about Everwhere but had also been there. It had been one of the first laws ever written: no human would be allowed to leave if she ever entered the land. "Why?" asked Ythoda, defiantly, hoping to find the matter up for discussion.

"You're a smart girl, Ythoda. You don't need to ask why; you know why."

Ythoda bowed her head, defeated. The Power was right, she didn't need to ask why; she understood completely that Everwhere needed to protect itself from humans knowing about it and that her visit made her a liability.

But still…but still…

"But how can you know I will tell? I don't even want to talk about…about all this!" Ythoda looked the Power in the eye, beseechingly, trying to communicate her earnest honesty, her firm resolution never to speak about what she had seen and experienced to anyone outside the Land. "I promise you, you are all safe from me. You must believe me!".

"I know that you will gladly promise not to tell. And that you will do everything you can to keep that promise," the Indigo lady spoke softly, soothingly. She could indeed see all the way into Ythoda's heart and knew she spoke the truth, at least as far as she knew. But she also knew that few truths are eternal in a human's mind and this she tried to communicate to the girl. " I know that, I believe you. But the thing is, that humans can hardly ever keep a promise such as the one you are making; no matter how important a secret, the burden usually becomes too great for them not to share. You are human Ythoda, even if you're not like most, and your nature would end up making you tell."

Ythoda shook her head, her eyes full of tears. Deep inside, she knew the Power was right, but she wasn't ready to give in, not if that meant saying goodbye to her former life forever.

" I'm telling you, I won't! I know it will be hard, but I am strong, I can do this, I know I can! I won't tell, really I won't, not ever I won't!"

"Maybe not now, maybe not for years, But sometime, you'll want to tell someone. To impress them perhaps, or just because you don't want to live with a secret any longer. Believe me," the Power added, seeing Ythoda shaking her head more and more emphatically. "You'd end up telling."

"No one would believe me anyway! They would think I was crazy and lock me up or something! I'd have to be really stupid to tell". Ythoda was yelling now, giving up all pretence of self- possession, hoping it would make the Power understand her, believe her, let her go. It didn't help.

Kindly, compassionately, the Power shook her head, stroking the girl's cheek, feeling her pain and wishing she could take it away. "You'd tell."

"But you said you were working on my wish! How can you say you're working on it and tell me I can't go home at the same time! Unless you're lying to me!"

The Power looked shocked- not because she found the accusation offensive but because she was literally incapable of lying. It takes an imagination to come up with a lie and imaginary beings…

She didn't try to explain this to Ythoda, though, seeing in her blazing eyes that she wouldn't be believed (despite her feeling for the child, the very thought amused the Power, though she had the sense not to show it). Instead, she explained that they were recreating Ythoda's hometown with everybody and everything in it just as it was in the real world. Ythoda could live there her whole life and she would never know the difference- in fact, the Powers would see to it that she forgot she wasn't really home. "It's the best we can do, child. But we'll make sure you are happy. We do want you to be happy, you know?"

Ythoda shook her head, looking down. What the Power was describing might look like the perfect solution from the outside, but it didn't convince her at all. The promises notwithstanding, she couldn't believe she'd ever be able to see her new life as anything but fake: fake town, fake friends, fake home, fake parents…Ythoda had always hated everything fake and the thought of going through her whole life like that almost made her sick with dread and longing; for the whole set-up might not look like she would be loosing anything, but she would be, she would most definitely be…

And there was something else there, something she couldn't quite put her finger on but that seemed even more important than her own feelings. Ythoda needed time, time to digest, time to accept or, if the knot in her throat and stomach didn't go away, time to come up with an alternate plan.

Slowly, she walked away from the Power and the Warden, away from Frank and George, away from the door.

She didn't go far, just a few hundred meters down the road, where a stone that looked just like a chair was waiting, warm in the sun, just for her to sit on. It hadn't been there before Ythoda wished for it.

The Power had the sense to make everyone leave her alone with her thoughts - better let the girl come to terms with her fate (which, as far as the Power was concerned, was a good one- after all, every one of Ythoda's wishes would come true from now on) at her own pace. There was no hurry.

No time is all the time in the world.

31

"**D**o the Powers want only <u>me</u> to be happy?"

The Power turned and looked into Ythoda's earnest face. "Is it only my happiness you care about or does other people's count as well?"

Actually, the purpose of Everwhere is not to provide happiness to people. The Land doesn't even have a purpose, it just is- much like any other country in the world; just because Everwhere is not in the world (at least, not in the way we understand that concept), it doesn't mean it must automatically exist to serve us humans, does it?

Still, people wish for things they think will make them happy. Granted, we often have no clue about what happiness really means- we usually never have a clue, actually. But that never has stopped any of us from pursuing happiness any way we can and wishing for it when we think we don't have it (even though more often than not, what will make us happy is already there, except we are too stubborn to see it).

Anyway, we wish in order to be happy and wishes are the strongest force in Everwhere.[48] So it was almost inevitable that caring about the happiness of human beings, of the "real" people, would be deeply ingrained in the beings imagination had created.

"No, of course it's not just your happiness we care about. We want everybody to be happy, inside Everwhere or outside it. But when it

---

[48] Of course, there are also the fears, the "what ifs" and other such things. But these are only the sauce, so to speak. It's wishes that make up the bulk of everything that exists in Everwhere.

comes to the people outside, there's nothing we can do about it- it's their imaginings that govern us, not the other way around."

" But what if you could do something about it?" Ythoda was looking straight into the Power's eyes now, and the steel in her gaze was just as strong as the steel in the woman's voice had been earlier. "What if your actions did affect the outside world and you were to make someone unhappy by doing something?"

"Well, then we'd have to refrain from doing it. Our laws forbid us to do anything that would cause unhappiness to people "outside". Though we have never done anything that would."

"Except that's just what you'd be doing if you kept me here."

"No dear, I told you we'd fix it so that you would think you were really home, with your real parents and your real friends."

"But I wouldn't, would I? Not really."

The Power shook her head, a little impatiently. Surely the girl understood by now… She was completely unprepared for what came next.

"I would be here, not there. I would be with fake parents, not my real ones. And maybe I wouldn't notice, but what about my real parents? What would they feel when I never came home? Or did you have a plan for that too?" The Power didn't even shake her head. She just stood and stared, hearing what the girl was saying but still not understanding the implications. "No, I didn't think so" Ythoda held up her hand, seeing that the Power was about to speak. "Oh, yes, I know, time doesn't pass here as it does there, so they would never notice" The Power let out a sigh of relief and opened her mouth to speak again, but Ythoda went on, unstoppable. "But does it really work like that? Or would I live my life here, growing up, getting a job and married and all that, and finally getting old and dying while time didn't pass out there? And meanwhile, my world would never go on, it would just be frozen in time? Forever? Wo…"

Ythoda could not go on. Her words stuck in her mouth, the thought too scary to pursue. Her world frozen forever just because she wasn't there? Her parents, her friends, the people she cared about, everything else, would they just stay suspended for all eternity, unmoving, hard like statues? Would their life never go on just because she had crossed a door? Was she destroying their futures for them? Had she?

She swallowed hard, trying to get rid of the knot in her throat and tried not to picture the thought. It was hard, very hard.

"Well, actually," the Power hesitated. She knew the answer to the question, of course, but it wasn't an easy answer to give to a child. And, she sensed, it was going to cause trouble. "No, not really. See, time hasn't really stopped for them, just for you. If you went back, you'd enter their time at the same point you left it, as if time had never passed at all. Which it wouldn't have, at least not in a straight line. Anyway, what would happen is that, when you die (and that will happen, as everything dies in Everwhere, just like in your world), your body will appear in your world because that is where it came from. A human body can't exist in Everwhere without a living mind keeping it here through it's own free will or being kept here by a spell, as will happen to you."

"Let me get this straight: I will live here, and then die, and then they will find my dead body at the same moment and…place I left from?" Ythoda's voice had become harsh, her face like stone. The Power nodded, in deep earnest, her eyes showing that she was beginning to understand what it all really meant, where Ythoda's questions were leading. "I see. And they wouldn't recognize me, so my parents would think I had disappeared…oh, you mean they would recognize me?"

"Yes," the lady's voice came out hesitantly, as if she couldn't believe she was hearing herself say it. "Your body will return to the same state it had before you entered Everwhere; it would just be your mind that will have gone."

"So my parents would think I was dead…they would think their daughter had died mysteriously or maybe even had been murdered. They would have to live the rest of their lives without me, missing me, wondering what happened to me…Taking all that into account, would you mind telling me how you are planning to keep them from being unhappy?"

There was triumph in Ythoda's face as she said it. Let the Powers deal with that.

32

T he Power flickered for a moment, as if she wasn't there just for a fraction of a second.

Which was exactly what had happened.

The Power had been stunned while Ythoda spoke; she had never realised the problem the child was presenting to her, nor had any of the other Powers. Just like would happen to us if we were confronted with a similar situation, they had sought a solution which seemed to cover everything, but completely forgotten about one small, yet essential detail: eventually, Ythoda would have to go back to her own world, be it dead or alive. And then…her time would go on without her. And she would be missed.

I wouldn't blame the Powers; time is difficult enough to handle when it's linear, never mind time that speeds up and slows down at one's own convenience, and goes in circles at that.

But now, she was presented with a problem that seemed unsolvable and saw no other option than to go running back (yes, literally- like lightning she could run) to the Palace and consult with the others.

So she seemed to flicker for a moment and then be inexplicably out of breath while five other figures appeared panting next to her: three men and two women, each wearing a different colour, all as dazzling as herself. Despite the display of strength she had just put on, despite the power she could feel running through her own body, Ythoda wanted to cringe; all seemed lost now, there was nothing she could do to save herself, to save her parents. Nothing she said would be of any avail anymore.

It was not that Powers meant her any harm; but she was convinced that they were going to go ahead with their plan no matter what, that that was why the Indigo lady had summoned them all. And it was clear as the light of day to Ythoda that there would be nothing she could do against all of them together: no matter her wishing power, which, as a human, she had here, and no matter how strong her arguments were, if they wanted to, they would be able to force her into anything they wanted…and make her happy about whatever it was they were doing to her while they were at it.

"I take it this is the girl who will make us change our laws" said the eldest of them, a tall, ebony skinned woman dressed in red, taking Ythoda's chin in her hand.

"The same" answered the Indigo Power.

The eldest Power smiled at her. "Child, you've caused us quite a headache. Nothing like this has ever happened to Everwhere and I don't mind telling you that we've had quite a fright over you. We just had no idea what to do until Green," here, she nodded towards a tall man dressed in green, who nodded back with a smile, "came up with this plan. How were we to know your logic would blow our idea to smithereens? And now, you're causing us a great deal of work too; you don't change the laws just like that in a place like this. There will be more than a few adjustments to be made…" She patted Ythoda on the cheek. "But don't worry, we're completely OK with that- clearly, when we made the law on human visitors we didn't really understand what the implications to them would be; and we were arrogant enough to believe we did know. Little girl, we have learnt a lot from you and we are grateful. It would seem that our heads were getting a bit too big for us." At this, the other five Powers burst out laughing, while Ythoda looked at them in astonishment; the last thing she would have expected of such regal people was for them to be happy about a kid like her teaching them a lesson. But apparently, they were; at least, they all beamed at Ythoda looking at her as if she had given them a great gift. One of them, a young man dressed in sky blue, even gave her a wink.

And Ythoda suddenly felt completely at ease. She looked at Frank, who had also lost the worried look he had been wearing since they first encountered the Wardens, and they smiled at each other. This was the last thing they would have expected from the situation; these Powers of Everwhere, the beings that everybody both adored and feared, weren't stern, haughty figures. Though they could do whatever they wanted to whomever they wanted to do it to, they didn't at all behave like they were high above everybody. Sure, they looked wise and powerful enough, but there was a twinkle in their eyes that made them impossible to fear; because who could fear people who had a sense of humour, and who were able to laugh at themselves and learn from their mistakes?

No one was angry with Ythoda; no one was going to take revenge on her for anything. In fact, they were even grateful to her for teaching them a lesson. Grateful! To her!

Ythoda took a deep, relieved breath. Everything was going to be all right.

"So, how do you think we should solve this?" Ythoda was baffled. She hadn't expected to be the one to come up with the solution to the problem, but the eldest Power had taken her apart and was now looking at her earnestly. "We obviously can't keep you here, but we still can't let you go around talking about Everwhere. I must confess we're a bit at loss here, so if you have any suggestions…".

Ythoda thought hard. She had thought at first that it would be easy to keep her adventure quiet and had even been offended when the first Power had said that her human nature would end up making her talk; but in her time thinking alone, she had admitted to herself that it was true.

"Can I wish on myself?" she asked. She could, but the wish wouldn't have any power outside Everwhere; once she was home, she would have to depend on willpower alone, and even though she had enough of that, it was not likely at all that it would keep her from spilling the beans about her adventure at some time or other.

"Anything I can do to help?"

As long as Ythoda was in danger of having to stay in Everwhere, Frank had kept to the background; it wasn't his battle, especially as for him there would have been no difference between leaving and staying.

But now they were definitely leaving, he felt it was his problem too and he wanted to help his sister get home as soon as she could. She had waited long enough.

He sat down next to her and put his arm around her shoulder. Ythoda welcomed the gesture, even though she would normally have put it down as "mushy". And then, as they both sat thinking together, the answer came as by magic. They looked up, looked at each other. Frank nodded. Ythoda stood up and marched to where the Red lady was standing; the Power listened intently, nodding approvingly as Ythoda spoke: right now, she didn't have any wish of telling about the Land, but if the time ever came when she was ready to discuss everything that had happened to her, something she very much doubted, she had Frank to talk to about it; after all, he knew Everwhere as intimately as could be, seeing as he came from there, and besides, he wasn't in a position to divulge any information, what with being invisible to the world and all.

"Oh, of course," the Red lady exclaimed, smiling broadly, her hand on Ythoda's shoulder. "We had all forgotten… You are not alone."

33

The park was flooded with sunshine, just as it had been when they left.

Everything else was also in place; there even were exactly the same people sitting on the benches as there had before, and the woman with the stroller hadn't quite finished passing by the door yet.

Frank and Ythoda stopped for just a moment, looking around, enjoying the view they had so longed to escape just that morning, loving everything about their boring, old, park,

And then, for once hand in hand, they ran home.

The woman at the bookstore waved at Ythoda as she ran past, the man from the ice-cream cart shouted a hello. As they turned the corner of the street where the baker was, the twins slowed down. There was a little figure playing on the sidewalk in front of the baker's shop.

Ythoda's heart raced for a moment as they walked up to the child. The little boy looked up to her and smiled.

"Look, I've got a new car".

"Wonderful." Ythoda patted his head and started down the street again, Frank running at her side.

There was their house, just where they left it. The window of their bedroom was open and they could hear the sound of a vacuum cleaner coming through it.

Ythoda sped up, leaving Frank to follow. He didn't try to catch up, knowing she needed to do this alone.

She rushed though the garden fence, over the path to the back door, opened and stormed in.

She didn't wipe her feet, she slammed the door, she shouted for her mother, she completely forgot her manners.

The vacuum cleaner stopped. Mum came down the stairs.

"Ythoda, what's this? Do you really have to yell like that? And don't tell me you have forgotten to wipe your feet again, you'll have to clear up the mess your..."

The stream of words from her mother stopped short as Ythoda rushed up to her and hugged her. Unseen to everybody but Ythoda, Frank was doing the same thing.

"I love you, Mum."

Ythoda laughed at her mother's astonished face- it was strange to say those words, but it felt marvellous.

Then, she went to wipe her feet and into the living room to pick up her coloured pencils and her sketching book.

After cleaning the dirt her shoes had left on the floor, she and Frank would go upstairs and finish their Lego castle.

Yesterday she had been complaining to him that everything about her life was too predictable, just too boring.

Today, she loved every single, predictable, boring detail of it.

Ythoda was home.